ADVANCE PRAISE FOR
SAY UNCLE

"*Say Uncle* starts like the best of coming-of-age story: one about family, young love, and identity. Then the rot rears its head. Cultists, murder, unwanted obligations, and your favorite uncle stealing your bedroom—then trying to sacrifice your girl. Bradley has dropped an absolute wrecking ball of a story. Thoroughly recommended."

—Zachary Ashford,
Australian Shadows-nominated
author of *Polyphemus*.

"*Say Uncle* is an inventive story of family, monsters, and the horrors that shape us. Blending imaginative gore, dark magic, and the childhood experiences that never truly fade, this story delivers both chills and heart. Packed with plenty of laughs and a big dose of adventure, *Say Uncle* is a wild ride."

—Celso Hurtado,
International Latino Award Winning
author of *The Ghost Tracks*

"*Say Uncle* is a wild cross-genre romp in which Ryan C. Bradley effectively uses nostalgia, humor, and evocative grotesqueries to deliver a unique angle on coming-of-age horror."

—Jessica McHugh,
3x Bram Stoker Award nominated
author of *The Train Derails in Boston*

"A viciously fun story of family dysfunction meeting dark magic."

—Johnny Compton
author of *The Spite House*

SAY UNCLE

RYAN C. BRADLEY

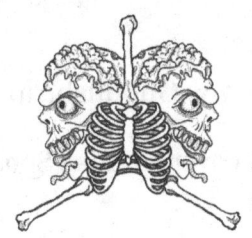

Ghoulish Books
San Antonio, Texas

Say Uncle
Copyright © 2025 Ryan C. Bradley

First Edition

All Rights Reserved

ISBN: 978-1-963801-10-1

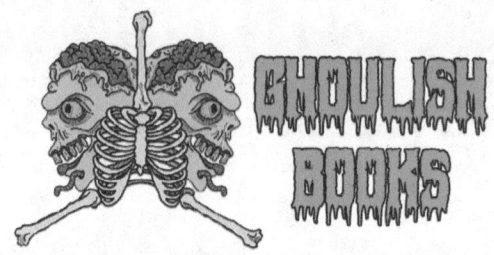

www.Ghoulish.rip

Front cover by Luke Spooner

Also by Ryan C. Bradley

Saint's Blood
Dumb Bullshit for Brilliant Idiots (co-author)
Bad Connections: Horror Stories

For all the kids out there struggling to break free of the bullshit. This book's for you.

Content Warnings

Say Uncle is a horror novel about the ways misogyny and toxic masculinity are passed down and enforced. That's some fucked up shit, and it's going to be ever present as you read.

You can also expect child abuse, neglect, and gnarly gore.

"a monster is just a man trying on his daddy's skin"

—Brionne Janae, "Confession"

CHAPTER 1

Away Message
BrayDay327: Not just HAGS. Going to have
the best one ever.

THE YEAR I turned five, I argued with another boy about whose brother was the worst. He had twin older brothers, one who hit and one who teased. Eventually we agreed that it was my brother, Sam. He did both. He throttled me so often that my parents moved his seat across the dinner table so he couldn't reach my neck while we were eating. Whenever I said something he thought was wrong, he punched my arm—driving his knuckle between the bicep and the bone. I had to wear long sleeves to cover the bruises. He honed in on everything he perceived as a mistake, down to writing songs about how much I liked chocolate ice cream.

My mother heard about my conversation, through the magical mother grapevine. When I got home, she took me upstairs to talk.

She told me, in no uncertain terms, that what I had done was wrong. I needed to look out for my family. The things I said about Sam would stay in other people's minds forever. A reputation couldn't be repaired.

Yet I write this now. By telling you this story, I'm breaking that cone of silence, and it's going to hurt the people I love. I'm spitting in the face of my family.

The year I turned fifteen, we took the Metro North into the city to see my Uncle Pauly and Aunt Linda in their Upper East Side apartment, above Wolf Pho Vietnamese Fusion. The five floors stretching above shared a lobby with the restaurant, so we had to pass the host booth to get to the staircase. My family—me, Sam, our sister Leslie, and our parents—climbed up.

Uncle Pauly and Aunt Linda's door opened into their kitchen, covered with my cousins' drawings of their favorite fireworks from the Fourth of July and a blue hand turkey that had somehow survived since Thanksgiving. The table separated Uncle Pauly and Aunt Linda. A beach scented candle burned low between them.

Aunt Linda popped out of her chair and hugged me, smushing my face into her chest. I wished that I was taller for a lot of reasons, but especially so I could avoid the uncomfortable feelings that came with having my face squished in my aunt's boobs. At least she moved on to Sam quickly.

For a second, Uncle Pauly sat like he'd just gotten out of timeout and if he kept his posture nice and straight then whatever he'd done would be really forgiven. He was an ex-tight end, and family lore held he would've made it to the NFL if his knee hadn't blown out his sophomore year of college. His hugs used to rattle me, but I'd graduated to a handshake and a slap on the back.

They put me through the regular battery of questions. How was school? Good. What was my favorite subject? Gym. Did I have a girlfriend? No. But any cute girls you might be talking to?

When I blushed, Aunt Linda said, "Pauly, stop." Usually, she'd squawk it, but there was something gentler there this time.

"All right, go see the kids," Uncle Pauly said.

Sam was seventeen, so he stayed with the adults, but me and Leslie went to the living room. She and Pauly's older kid Maria were both ten. Maria and her younger brother Paul Jr. were plopped down on the couch in front of the TV watching a show about pickup artists. "We need to show you upstairs," Maria told me and my sister.

"Upstairs?" I asked. Their apartment was a rectangle. The door opened into the kitchen, which fed into Maria's bedroom, which fed into the living room. It shared a wall with the study, which fed into Paul Jr.'s room parallel to Maria's, which fed into Uncle Pauly's and Aunt Linda's room, parallel to the kitchen. There were no stairs.

"Mom and Dad bought the apartment upstairs," Maria said.

"Really?"

"Yes. Ms. Harriet slit her wrists in the tub. Mom and Dad asked the building owner to rent her place at the funeral," she said, a little too cheerfully.

"Daddy says that's how hard it is to find an apartment in the city," Paul Jr. said.

"Let's go," Leslie said.

The kids marched past the kitchen table. "Mom, we're going upstairs to Daddy's room," Maria said.

The adults barely looked up.

"Make sure the kids don't get into anything they're not supposed to, Braden," Uncle Pauly shouted after us.

The layout of the upstairs apartment followed the intestinal shape of the downstairs with each room feeding into the next, but there were no carpets, no paintings, no pictures, no life. The hardwood floors warped upward. A queen-sized bed pressed against the wall in the second room. Shadows gathered in the corners in defiance of the overhead lights. A draft shuddered through the apartment.

"Echo!" Paul Jr. yelled, even though there really wasn't one.

"Do you want to see the room where Ms. Harriet died?" Maria asked.

"No," I said, but Paul Jr. had me by the wrist and Leslie was pushing me from behind.

"It took them weeks to clean up the blood," Maria said, as she opened the bathroom door.

"They had to use special cleaners," Paul Jr. said.

Whoever scrubbed it did a good job. From what I could tell, it was a regular New York City bathroom with a white tub, a toilet, and a sink cramped together, leaving a tiny square for a small person to stand. The mirror hung across from the toilet so you would have to look yourself in the eye while you shat.

"Do you think there's a ghost?" Leslie asked.

"There's no such thing as ghosts," I said.

"Mommy says there is," Paul Jr. said.

"I've seen her eyes looking back at me in the mirror," Maria said, matter-of-factly.

"What do they look like?" Leslie asked.

"Stop," I said. "You're going to give yourselves nightmares." Of course they ignored me. They didn't listen and I'd be the one to get in trouble.

"Her eyes are brown," Maria said. "Mine are blue, but when I look in the mirror I see her eyes instead of mine."

"I've seen it too," Paul Jr. said.

They dragged me into the kitchen.

"This would be perfect for hide and go seek," Leslie said.

"Braden's it!" Paul Jr. and Maria yelled at once.

"Close your eyes and count to one hundred," Leslie said.

"Oh, and no one is allowed to go on the right side of the apartment. Everyone has to hide on this side," Paul Jr. said. "That's Daddy's rule."

"This isn't a good idea," I said, but the three of them were already scurrying away. There was no furniture, so I didn't know where they thought they would hide, but I closed my eyes and pretended to count.

I didn't want to step another foot into the place. But I

didn't want them to see me balk, either. They were going to have to live here. "Ready or not, here I come!"

There wasn't any sign of them, and I felt someone watching me. I spun in a slow circle. No one was there. Goosebumps popped up on the back of my neck. The temperature in the upstairs apartment seemed to plummet.

I wanted to find the kids quickly, but instead I walked slowly, checking on my sides and behind me as I progressed. The paint peeling off the baseboards and the archways without doors didn't leave space for the kids to hide, yet I couldn't see them.

I creeped under the first archway. Someone giggled behind a closet door. I snuck over and grabbed the knob. One of them was inside.

I twisted and pulled. Even knowing what was coming, I fell on my back, a cry choking in my throat, when Paul Jr. jumped out yelling.

He laughed like it was the funniest thing he'd ever seen.

"Braden, do you want to see something cool?"

Before I could say no, he was guiding me into the closet. It had a separate exit on the other side of the apartment. "I know we're not supposed to go onto this side, but look at this," he said, and opened the door.

A mossy smell assaulted my nostrils. The temperature dropped a degree, maybe two. He guided me into the room by the hand.

I could've stopped him—I was bigger, older—but I was too stunned. We emerged in a dark room. The only light carried through the closet and lit the small section we were standing in, before being devoured by the shadows. I reached back for the wall, hoping against hope that the light switch would be on this side.

"Don't turn on the lights," Paul Jr. said. He disappeared into the darkness. There was no way I would've followed him.

5

I touched something with a texture like the exoskeleton of a cockroach. I jerked my hand away and swallowed a gag.

"Paul?' I said, whispering.

If I didn't bring him back, Uncle Pauly would kill me.

"Paul," I said, louder. I grabbed at the frame of the closet door, needing to touch something real. Whatever this was, it wasn't Narnia.

"Look at this, Braden." My cousin emerged from the shadows with a knife.

Something moved in the darkness. It sounded like a vine being dragged out of a bush. I pressed my back against the wall. Fear froze me.

When I unstuck myself, I said, "Let's take it back to the other room, with the light." I put my hands up to smack the knife away, just in case.

"Okay." He led me back into the closet.

"What was in there, Paul?"

He held up the knife. The blade extended straight for four of those inches like a standard paring knife before curving back into a triangular point at the tip.

"Check out the handle." It was bone white. I had to squint to make it out in the relative darkness, but once I saw it, the shapes were unmistakable. The handle was cobbled together from shrunken skulls.

"I've got to put it back."

Before I could grab him, he was gone. Something shook me from behind. I spun, and I threw a small body into the wall.

My sister screamed.

I had my fists up, ready to fight. I was shaking. Leslie glared from the floor.

"Is he in there again?" Maria asked from outside. "Dad is going to be so mad."

Paul Jr. pushed past me, knife nowhere to be seen. "No. I was only in the closet."

"What the hell, Braden," Leslie said, climbing off the floor.

SAY UNCLE

"Don't sneak up on me."

Maria imitated my ready pose and Leslie chortled. At least if Leslie was laughing I wouldn't get into trouble.

The apartment door opened and I jumped again.

Maria mimicked my pose, legs wide, fists up. This time Leslie and Paul Jr. did, too.

"Pizza's here," Uncle Pauly said.

CHAPTER 2

Away Message
EnterSamMan88: WTF!?!?!? The little turd is going to be sleeping on my floor all summer. Worst. Parents. Ever.

AT DINNER, the adults drank until they laughed at jokes that weren't funny. I wasn't allowed to have any alcohol, but Uncle Pauly gave Sam a beer. Sam's eyes bugged out when he drank and the adults laughed even harder.

Uncle Pauly slapped him on the back and said, "You're going to have to pretend to like it in college."

Sam was only applying to Ivys. Mom had gone to Princeton, so that was his number one.

The rest of the conversation repeated from our introductions. How's school? What's your favorite subject? Do you have any girlfriends?

Before I knew it, it was time to go. I went to hug Uncle Pauly goodbye, but he held up an arm. "We're going to the same place, buddy."

"But I'm leaving," I said, trying to clear up his confusion.

"You didn't tell him?" he asked my parents.

"We were going to talk about it when we got home," Dad said.

"Talk about what?" I asked.

Aunt Linda sighed. "Always secrets in this family. Did you think he wasn't going to notice?"

8

SAY UNCLE

"Uncle Pauly is coming to stay with us for a while," Mom said.

Sam jammed his knuckles into my thigh and whispered, "Stop asking questions."

I knocked his hand away. "Where's he going to sleep?"

"You're going to be on an air mattress," Mom said.

"In Sam's room," Dad added.

"What?" Sam asked. "No one said he was going to be in my room."

"Did you tell them anything?" Aunt Linda asked.

On the train back to Milford, two hours north of the city, my parents and Uncle Pauly sat in a row opposite Sam and Leslie, playing Extreme Uno. I shirked the spot between Sam and Leslie for an empty bench to curl up with my Game Boy. It was too dark to see the screen, but I wasn't really focused on it, anyway. At first, I obsessed about the apartment: the mossy smell, the wall that had felt so strange, and the glean of the knife's point. But those problems lived in New York City. The upstairs apartment shrank in my mind.

The train chugged toward my problems. At Boy Scouts camp the week before, I'd bribed one of the counselors to buy me a *Penthouse* in town. The magazine was hidden in the desk in my room under a pencil case and my notes from freshman year. Uncle Pauly might be cool if he found it. But he might tell Mom. My most pressing issue was how much trouble was I going to be in. I foresaw Dad taking the Xbox away, Mom dragging me to Mass every morning.

The battery on my Game Boy died. I slipped it into my backpack. I was hungry, and I knew my mother had packed six granola bars, six apples, and six bottles of water with initialed caps so we could refill them, but I didn't want to talk to her. She gave away my room.

Dad slid into the seat next to mine. "How's it going, Bray?"

"Good, my Game Boy just died and I have no room for the summer."

"Yeah," he said, as if these events had occurred naturally, out of his control. I'd told him every day for the last year that I'd hated him for making me go to an all-boys high school. He and my mother had offered me a choice between the public school and the private one. When I picked the public school, they told me it wasn't my choice.

"So they're getting divorced?"

My mother slid in next to my father. "Don't say that so loud." She looked around the train car. 10pm on a Tuesday was too late for the work commuters and too early for the drinkers but she acted as though it were jam-packed with familiar faces.

"Why not?" I asked.

"Because people are going to judge your uncle. We're a family. We look out for our own."

I wanted to ask what about me, when was it my turn to be looked out for? But I wasn't about to cry on a train, even an empty one.

"It's just going to be until he's back on his feet," Dad said.

"It'll be like camping," Mom said.

"Why didn't you tell me before?" I asked. "Did you think I wasn't going to notice Uncle Pauly sleeping in my room? What's wrong with the upstairs apartment he's renting?"

My parents exchanged a look, like they'd raised the world's biggest asshole.

"We thought you were a little young to understand," Mom said.

So they'd discussed it but decided I couldn't handle it. Great. "I'm fifteen." My mouth was dry. I rushed past fury, into a numb space.

"We know," Dad said.

SAY UNCLE

"I want a granola bar. A chocolate one."

Mom checked her bag. "I can give you an Apple Crisp or a Sweet Oats N' Honey. Sam ate both chocolate ones."

"Can you please just go away?"

"I just want to make sure you're okay," Dad said.

"Of course I am. You made me go to an all-boys school then gave away my bedroom. Why wouldn't we be okay?"

"I can see you're angry, so I'll go back to my seat," Dad said.

"Stay there," I said.

The vacuum roared as it filled the air mattress. The mattress was rounded at the corners, so the fitted sheet kept slipping off. Air wheezed out every time I rolled over, so I tried to lay still. At least Sam's room had an air conditioner.

The house was too old for central air, so my parents bought window units for their room downstairs, plus every other bedroom upstairs except mine. They said if I was warm, I could sleep on Sam's floor. It was another sore spot between us, that Sam and Leslie got air conditioners, but I didn't. I was a bitter kid before any of this. Some of it was puberty, but I remembered what happened when my parents let us pick our rooms. There were two big bedrooms and a small one in the upstairs hallway and we chose in birth order. Sam picked the biggest room in the center of the hall. My parents pitched the small room to me, highlighting how many toys could fit in the closet. When I still wanted the bigger one, it stopped being a choice. Mom needed to share a closet with Leslie.

"Don't make a big thing about this," Sam said. He propped himself up on an elbow, his bed frame looming over my air mattress.

"What?"

"Mom is being a good sister. We've got to come

together as a family and take care of Uncle Pauly. Did you hear what happened to his restaurant?"

"No," I said, but I had an idea. His restaurant had been close to the World Trade Center and some insurance companies refused to pay out after Bush had declared the attack an Act of War, but I was missing details. "Tell me."

"You're too young. Just be nice to him. Not everything is about you."

"I didn't even say anything."

"Lights out." Sam clicked off the lamp by his bed.

"I'm not ready."

"My room, my rules."

In the darkness, I caught a whiff of the mossy smell from Uncle Pauly's apartment.

CHAPTER 3

Away Message
BrayDay327: BRB. Finally getting an air conditioner. 2Cool4School.

I WOKE SHORTLY after seven. I was still snapped into the rhythm of camp. My troop had to start the mile hike at 7:30 to make it to the mess hall by 8 sharp. Being late meant not eating. I listened for signs of life.

The kitchen was below the kids' bedrooms, so I could make out Dad, Uncle Pauly, and Mom's muffled voices, though not what they were talking about. Mom's spoon scraped against the side of her teacup as she stirred. Sam snored lightly next to me. He woke up explosively angry, swinging at whatever he could reach. I guessed that Uncle Pauly was the lesser of the two evils.

For a second I thought about stepping into my room and grabbing the *Penthouse*, but where would I have put it? I didn't exactly have a lot of real estate in Sam's room: the air mattress, the sheet, and my body. So I headed downstairs.

Our house had two half staircases instead of one big one, so you had to walk down from the kids' bedrooms to the main floor containing the living room and my parents' room, then another half staircase to the kitchen.

"There he is," Uncle Pauly roared as I turned the corner. My parents were in their robes, but Pauly was in a white t-shirt and a pair of yellow boxer shorts.

"Good morning," I said.

13

"What would you like for breakfast?" Mom asked even though everything we had—a box of Cheerios, a container of frozen English muffins, and another box of high fiber cereal somehow more bland than Cheerios—was already laid out on the table. I grabbed a muffin and stuck it in the microwave.

"Braden, how do you sleep at night?" Uncle Pauly asked.

I froze. He knew that Paul Jr. had been on the wrong side of the apartment. Or he'd found my *Penthouse*.

My mom unhelpfully relayed the defrosting instructions, "30 seconds on power level 4."

The buttons of the microwave beeped and it buzzed on.

"You know what I mean," Uncle Pauly said.

I was sure my *Penthouse* was going in the trash and I'd be doing penance at 8 am Mass every morning for the rest of the summer.

"What do you mean?" Dad asked. His bathrobe was the same frayed, aquamarine one he'd been wearing since 1982.

"I can't believe you haven't told them," Uncle Pauly said.

I turned around. Everyone was looking at me, expectantly. They weren't angry yet, but they were about to be. There had been a brief moment the afternoon before as I showered off the grime of a week of camping where I had thought this was going to be the best summer of my life. Now that thought finished circling the toilet.

The microwave chirped behind me.

"His mattress is like a rock," Uncle Pauly said. "I've slept on stone slabs softer than that thing."

Oh, thank fuck.

"Braden, is that true?" my mom asked.

"And why doesn't he have an air conditioner? The other two kids have one," Uncle Pauly said.

"He can sleep on Sam's floor," Dad said. "Air conditioners aren't cheap."

SAY UNCLE

"The poor kid's going to get scoliosis *and* malaria at this rate. What's it, a hundred bucks, for an air conditioner?"

"Electricity isn't free," Dad said. He swirled the remnants of milk around his cereal bowl.

"Why didn't you tell us your mattress was so hard?" Mom asked.

"It's the only mattress I've ever slept on," I said.

"Of course he doesn't notice that it feels like a rock. He was sleeping on the ground for seven nights," Uncle Pauly said.

"Six," my mother corrected.

I cut my English muffin in two and buttered the fluffy half, then the crispy.

"Do you want to buy an air conditioner for the room?" Dad asked, jaw clenched.

"Yes. Hurry up, Braden. I'm getting dressed and then we're going to the hardware store."

"In what car?" Dad said.

"Yours." He slapped Dad on the back. "Thanks for offering."

Dad looked like steam was about to come out of his ears, and I for one couldn't be happier to see it.

Uncle Pauly went upstairs.

I scarfed down the soft side of my muffin with a glass of OJ. My parents looked at each other like they wanted some privacy.

"I have to eat here," I said. "We're not allowed to eat upstairs."

Mom said, "You're right, sweetie. Why didn't you tell us your mattress was hard? How can we fix something if we don't know it's a problem?"

I bit into the crunchy side—the better half.

"The mattress is fine," Dad said.

"I didn't know it was hard," I said between bites. I loved the feeling of butter against my lips almost as much as the taste of it.

15

"But we want to help you," Mom said. "You know that."

"So you didn't know that there was no air conditioner there? It really seems like Uncle Pauly wants to help me."

"He loves you. He's your Godfather," Mom said.

"Does he know that?" Dad asked, before leaving the table.

Once I finished my muffin, I followed suit.

I didn't want to keep Uncle Pauly waiting. I don't know if I could've put it into words then, but I can now: Uncle Pauly is incredibly charming when he wants to be. Ask any of his ex-wives and they'll tell you that, at a certain point, the charm turns off.

The girl behind the register at the hardware store was an Indian girl I'd gone to middle school with. We'd been in the same honors classes, but we'd both been so shy that we'd never actually spoken to one another.

"What about her?" Uncle Pauly asked.

"What do you mean?" I asked.

"You said you never got to talk to any girls because you went to an all-boys high school. Why don't you go talk to her?"

"I mean, she works here." She wasn't my type either. There wasn't anything wrong with her, but she was rail thin and at fifteen my only metric for attraction was cup-size.

"Just go over there and ask her for her phone number."

He led me down an aisle full of hammers, then mallets hanging on plastic hooks.

"I don't want to." My chest tightened.

"Worst thing that can happen is she says no."

We kept walking, into an aisle full of hacksaws.

"We have to check out, anyway. I'll introduce you."

"No," I said.

We got to the end of the store, where the air conditioners were stacked. A sign instructed us to ask an employee for assistance, but Uncle Pauly bear-hugged a window unit. I tried to help him, but there was nowhere for me to grab it.

"C'mon," he said.

I followed him through an aisle filled with nails.

"Don't say anything," I said.

"Too late," Uncle Pauly said as he slammed the air conditioner down in front of the register. The girl jumped.

"You aren't supposed to lift those," she said.

"Don't worry, I'm big and strong." He put a hand between my shoulder blades and pushed me forward. "This is my nephew. He's big and strong, too."

"Hi Braden," she said.

Great. She remembered my name and I didn't remember hers. "Hey! How are things at Foran?" I asked, hoping to deflect.

"They're okay. It's weird not seeing you in class anymore."

"Yeah. It's weird not having girls at school."

She scanned the air conditioner and turned to Uncle Pauly. "Cash or credit?"

"Cash. Do you know if that ice cream place up the road is any good?" He pulled out his billfold.

"Scoopy Doos? It's great."

"So you like ice cream?" he asked.

She squinted at him as she took the cash. "I love ice cream."

"Because Braden loves ice cream. too. And he'd be happy to buy you some when you have a break."

Her eyes widened as she turned to me. I blushed, as if to confirm.

Uncle Pauly nudged me.

"Yeah. That would be cool," I said.

"What about noon tomorrow?" she said.

"I need to talk to—"

"He'll be there," Uncle Pauly said, and took his change. He hefted up the air conditioner and led me out of the store. I couldn't stop smiling. I had my first date.

We dropped the air conditioner in the backseat of the car and then got some celebratory ice cream.

"See? That wasn't so bad, was it?" He swung his ice cream cone as he spoke.

My cheeks were sore from grinning.

"You gotta listen to me," he said.

I ate a spoonful of my Rocky Road.

"We're not just here to eat. We're scoping out the location."

Scoopy Doos was next to the dock, across a walking bridge from the library, where people parked their cars and walked to the train station to save a few bucks. There was a patio for the Historical Society with white umbrellas.

"Get a table. One with an umbrella. Ask her if the sun's getting in her eyes, and then you don't wait for an answer. Open the umbrella. You're showing her that you're the man. You call the shots."

I took a bite of my ice cream, trying to get an even ratio of marshmallow to almond.

"Are you listening, Braden? I'm not telling you twice."

"Yes, get a table, open the umbrella before she asks."

"Wrong. You're asking, then opening. You're showing her who the boss is right away."

"Sir, yes sir."

"Very funny. Then you talk about whatever kid shit you're into for a while. At the end of your date, brush her hair back behind her ear, pause while you look her in the eye, then kiss her."

"Shouldn't I ask first?"

"Do you want her to say no?"

"No."

"Then don't ask." He took a big lick from his cone. "And another thing, you get a cone tomorrow, not a cup."

"Why?" I asked, not really wanting to know the answer.

"Because the cup is for pussies. People who aren't man

enough to manage the melt. You're going to ask her for her phone number, not set up another date."

"Why?" Was there any portion of my date that I was going to plan?

"Because once you have her phone number, you're going to make her wait."

"I don't want to hurt her feelings." I imagined the pit that would form in my stomach, as I waited for the phone to ring.

"Do you want her to want you or not? It's a dance. You tell them you like them, then you take it away. You make them feel special, and then you take it away. It's irresistible."

"Huh."

"And remember, this is practice."

"What?"

"You might think you're falling in love, but you gotta remember that you're learning how to play the game. Once you get it, you dump her and move on to someone hotter."

My parents were sending me to an all-boys school to avoid "distractions," which in their minds translated to sex, but really meant healthy relationships with girls. The little understanding I had of girls came from sitcoms, Leslie, and now Uncle Pauly.

CHAPTER 4

Away Message
BrayDay327: Maybe this will be the best summer ever!!! Can't say anything yet, but <3 :)

UNCLE PAULY COULD lug the air conditioner up the stairs by himself, but he needed me to hold the window open. A centerfold of Jimi Hendrix playing at Woodstock clipped from a music magazine was taped to one wall, and a KISS tapestry I'd bought at a state fair hung on another. My room was the smallest in the house, with a slim space to walk in between the dresser, bed, closet, and an antique desk where I'd hid my *Penthouse* that opened upward.

Uncle Pauly had draped yesterday's shirt over the desk, so he probably hadn't put anything inside it. The shirt answered another question as well: it must be where the mossy smell had come from last night.

After we'd gotten the air conditioner installed, I took some of my clothes to hang in the section Mom had cleared for me in Sam's closet. Later that day, Dad bought some plastic drawers for me to empty my dresser into.

When I'd finished, I walked up the hill to my friend Joel's house. His name was pronounced the Spanish way, Jo-el. He broke his wrist falling over the handlebars of his bike the month before. He was obsessed with the song, "Handlebars," and every time he sang about being able to ride a bike with no handlebars I said, "No you can't," and pointed to the cast around his wrist.

SAY UNCLE

"What's good, dude?" he said when he opened the door. He lived with his mom and grandparents. He was my height but a hundred pounds heavier and built like a Mack truck from lifting boxes of apples at Shop & Stop. He was half Puerto Rican and looked it, while I was a quarter Mexican but looked mayonnaise-white. That was at least a part of why we were friends.

"Life's been crazy. You remember my uncle Pauly?"

"He's the big one. Kind of an asshole?"

"That's him. He moved into my house. I got a *Penthouse* hidden in my desk."

"Just one?" he asked. He led me to his room. There was a giant Beatles poster from his weekends-and-holidays-only Dad over the bed and a layer of dirty laundry so thick that you could only tell the floor was hardwood by feel. He fished in between some jeans and tossed me a *Playboy*. From underneath a shirt, he got a *Hustler*. He reached under his pillow and handed me an older *Penthouse*.

A pair of blonde twins on the cover were frozen the moment before they'd kiss, the model in front's breast eternally about to pop out of her bra.

"You look like a missionary standing there like Jehovah's about to witness his first titty," Joel said.

I put down the magazines and sat on the corner of the bed. He didn't have any chairs. "Where did you get all of these?"

"I asked my mom."

"What?!" If I'd asked my mother, I'd be living off the body of Christ until I moved out.

"My mom's cool, dude." He flopped on the bed, a solid foot away from me. The impact bounced me.

Outside, his mom yelled, "Joel, you seen my keys?"

"Ignore her, she'll find them," Joel said.

I held up the magazine so the centerfold with the blonde twins bounced out. "Lucky you. I got to get it before my uncle finds it."

"Okay. That's easy. Wait for him to go out." He scratched at the skin under his cast.

21

"Then where do I put it? I'm sleeping in Sam's room."

"You think he wouldn't like it?"

"Not as much as he'd like to get me in trouble."

"Your brother is awesome. Do you remember the Lego truck?"

Of course I did. Joel and I had tied a Lego rescue truck to a ceiling fan and turned the fan on to see if the rope could hold it. It did, the truck spinning around the room like a brick. When we showed Sam, he put me in a Nelson and held me until the truck shattered against my jaw. The bricks scattered across the room, leaving the rope to whip through the air on its own.

"If Sam's going to rat you out, bring it here. My mom doesn't care." She was still yelling about her keys in the background.

"Okay."

"I won't even get the pages sticky."

"You're gross." I threw a pillow at him. "But get this, you remember the tall Indian girl from my science class?"

Joel and I had never been in the same classes. He was dyslexic ("That means he can't rade," I told anyone who would listen) and now he was going to an Agriscience program at a public high school two towns over.

"The one who works at the hardware store? The hot one?"

"Yeah. I've got a date with her and I don't know her name."

Joel sat up. "How did you ask her out if you don't know her name?"

"Uncle Pauly basically did it for me."

"He's the fucking man!" Joel clapped once, then rubbed the cast around his wrist. "What are you going to do?"

His mom barged into the room without knocking. "Joel, did you not hear me? Where the fuck are my keys?"

"Mom, Braden has a date with a girl but he doesn't know her name."

22

SAY UNCLE

"How do you not . . . I don't have time for this. Congratulations, Bray. Be yourself and don't waste time playing stupid games," she said to me, then turned to her son. "Joel, I'm going to be late for work."

"Have you checked under your pillow?"

Joel's mom slapped her thigh. "Damnit." As quickly as she'd swept in, she was gone.

"But seriously, what're you going to do about finding out this girl's name?"

"I was hoping you'd know."

Joel's mom slammed the front door, apparently with the keys, then peeled out of the driveway.

"Shit," Joel said.

"You know anyone we can ask who won't tell her?"

"MySpace."

Joel's family's computer was in his grandparents' bedroom, with an alarmingly pink decor. The sheets on the bed, the curtains, the walls. His grandfather drank vodka all day and his grandmother coped with pink.

"Grandpa. Can we use the internet to look up a girl's name?"

Joel's dial-up meant we had to take the phone off the hook and listen to the strange series of beeps and buzzes before we could get on. My family had broadband by then, but our one computer was in the kitchen and I had to wait for a turn. When it finally came up, someone would always be there, looking over my shoulder. Uncle Pauly knew about the date, obviously, but I'd prefer if the rest of my family didn't. Sam had enough ammunition.

"Does she go to your school?" Joel's grandpa barely moved his mouth when he talked, like a ventriloquist without a dummy.

"She did," I said.

"Why don't you use your yearbook?"

Joel didn't have one, but my mother had insisted that we buy one every year and it was under my bed. Two birds, one stone.

CHAPTER 5

Away Message
bigRican787: Dial up succccckkkkkksssssssss. But not as much as your mom! Be here for the next two minutes.

NEITHER CAR WAS in our driveway when I returned home. "Hello?" I called, head poking through the door before fully entering. The breakfast dishes that didn't fit in the dishwasher were upside down on the drying rack. Neither TV was on. Maybe I'd caught a lucky break. Joel's shift started at 2, so I wouldn't be able to drop the magazine off until the next day. But still, I tiptoed up the stairs. With six people in the house, there was never telling when anyone might pop out.

There was no one in the living room when I crested the top of the first set of stairs. All the doors were closed on the second flight. My mother and I were engaged in a silent battle over those doors. I liked them closed so no one could jump out and stab me without opening a door, but she wanted to let the light flow.

I put my ear against the door to my room.

There was no hum from the AC. Still, I turned the knob quietly, half-expecting to see Uncle Pauly sleeping on my bed.

With the door cracked, the heavy stench of moss assaulted my nostrils. The same thing we'd smelled back at his apartment, only much stronger now.

I'd been pushing the upstairs and the knife from the

closet out of my head, whether I realized it or not. The smell was too weird to place. Mossy, yes, but mixed with something else. That other element was something rare, like a new form of knowledge. Or maybe, a very old one.

But either way, I could still picture the boobs in the pages of that *Penthouse* and I wanted to see them again. I slipped through the door. The blinds, which I always kept closed, were open. The window overlooked the driveway, so I could see if anyone came home.

I crept farther. Then I reached under Uncle Pauly's shirt and lifted the desktop enough to slip a hand in. Instead of the glossy cover of a magazine, I touched something dry and husky, like discarded skin. I ripped my hand back. The desktop clapped shut. My eyes watered as I fought back a gag.

I lifted the top again and knelt so I could see into the desk. The thing I'd touched was a book. I could almost laugh at myself for being so stupid. I loved books.

I grabbed it with my index finger and my thumb and held it up to get a better look. Touching it gave me the same cold panic as a cockroach crawling up my leg.

The jacket was bound with something leathery, the color of coffee stains on clean paper. Nothing on the spine. I dropped it onto the desk.

"What is this?" I whispered.

I opened it to the red ribbon saving Uncle Pauly's spot. The text wasn't written in a western alphabet, but there was a diagram on the page. In it, a person in a robe held up a knife like the one Paul Jr. had shown me, with the skulls on the handle and the blade pointing backward. The robed individual stood above a naked woman tied on a marble slab. A monster loomed over them.

Its limbs were thick, arms and legs the same size as the man in the diagram's torso. Little twirls all around made the monster's skin resemble moss despite the lack of color. Its head wasn't a human oval but a half moon. In the absence of a neck, the head stuck out of the shoulders like an egg being swallowed by a snake. The eyes were big, nearly the size of its hands. It didn't have a mouth or a nose, at least that I could see in the diagram.

The next page was all gibberish, neither the straight, certain letters of Latin characters or the curly figures of the Cyrillic alphabet. Something I'd never seen before. I needed to find a way to translate it, because this couldn't be right. This couldn't be Uncle Pauly's book. Not the same guy who had gotten me a date, bought me an air conditioner, then taken me for ice cream all in the same day. Putting it maybe too simply, this book was evil. I wasn't allowed to watch horror movies, but I'd caught a few at Joel's house, and this book was the kind of thing that the drunk teenagers read aloud with perfectly accented Latin after fucking and accidentally summoned a demon.

I leafed through the pages. More nonsense. Nothing in Latin. And then another diagram. This one was a close-up of the naked woman's chest with a line indicating where to stab through the ribs to hook the heart.

He'd only packed one duffle bag to stay with us and he'd decided to bring this.

A car door slammed in the driveway. I couldn't hear what he was saying, but I recognized Uncle Pauly's voice. I dropped down so he wouldn't see me in the window.

Shit.

Downstairs, a key turned in the lock. I returned the book and grabbed the *Penthouse*.

"Hello," Uncle Pauly said.

"Is there anybody home?" Leslie shouted.

I hid the magazine underneath my shirt. The yearbook!

The TV turned on downstairs. I was safe. Then I heard the theme music for *The Powerpuff Girls*.

Uncle Pauly creaked on the first stairwell.

I scrambled to the floor where I'd left the yearbook, but Uncle Pauly's duffle bag was on top of it.

I dug around beneath his bag until I found the

yearbook. With it in hand, I rushed out into the hall. Uncle Pauly cut me off at the landing.

"Hey, Braden. What do you got there?"

He backed me into his room, guiding me down onto the bed. I hugged the yearbook to my chest over the stiff magazine.

When he sat down next to me, the mattress sunk. I had to focus to not slide into him.

"I know this used to be your room, Braden. But I can't have you going through my belongings."

I nodded. "I needed to get my yearbook. I don't know the name of the girl from the hardware store."

He paused, as if in deep consideration. "Where was it?"

"Underneath your duffel bag." Nowhere near the creepy book in my desk.

"Bray, this can't be a thing. From now on, if you need to get something from this room, you're going to have to ask my permission. I'm going to have to come with you."

"I understand."

He eyed me, closely. "Did you see anything else?"

I tried not to make a face. "No."

"Nothing in my desk?"

"No, didn't go near the desk." I hugged the yearbook tighter to the magazine hidden underneath my shirt. My sweat pasted the cover to my skin.

"Why all the sneaking if this was just for the yearbook?"

I had never been a good liar. "I didn't think it was a big deal."

"I haven't been going through your things. Would you like it if I was digging around in your closet?"

"No. It won't happen again."

"No, it won't. Tomorrow, when I take you for your date, I'm going to buy a lock for this door and I'm going to have the only key."

"That's a good idea." I traced the pattern of the hardwood floor with my eyes.

"What is it that you're not telling me? I ran restaurants for twenty years. Do you know how many waitresses have tried to lie to me? They were trying to make it on Broadway, and they were better at acting than you."

I compromised. Better to lose the magazine than to acknowledge the book. The cover of my *Penthouse* squelched as I let it peel off my chest.

Uncle Pauly examined it. This was going to be bad. Sam would sing songs about me masturbating. Leslie would call me a pervert. Dad would tell me how disappointed he was. Mom would be the worst.

Uncle Pauly chortled. "This is what all the sneaking was about. Where was this baby hidden?" He held the magazine open by the backcover. The centerfold bounced out. He nodded appreciatively.

"It was tucked in the cover of the yearbook."

"Clever." His focus remained on the centerfold's spread legs.

"You're not going to tell my mom, are you?" I asked.

He closed the magazine. "How about this? I get the lock. I don't tell anybody. And you promise that you're not going to sneak into this room again."

"Deal."

He handed me the *Penthouse*. "Forget about the pictures. Read the letters section. You can learn some good shit."

CHAPTER 6

Away Message
BrayDay327: Yoooo. Saw something really messed up. Might be off the computer for a while.

LOOK: I WAS a stupid kid. I did fine in school, but the riptide of raging hormones drowned me when it came to anything else. There my uncle was, hiding books with sketches diagramming how to sacrifice a human being, but I didn't tell anyone because it might clue them into the fact that I, a fifteen-year-old boy, masturbated. Instead of talking to my parents, I hid my *Penthouse* in my pillowcase.

Sure I thought about the book. I wondered whether or not it could actually do anything. Like, if Uncle Pauly really cut someone's heart out, what would happen next? The police would come, put him away for the rest of his life, but what else? I imagined him shooting fireballs out of his hands, raising an army of undead zombies, collecting a pile of treasure that would fill an entire room in his apartment. Whenever I did think about it, I diverted my thoughts the best I could to my date.

I found her face next to Joel's in the yearbook. Mancinas next to Matthew. Ancy Matthew. In school, I hadn't given her a second look, but now that I had a date with her, I was seeing her for the first time. How had I missed the spark in her brown eyes? Or the way her black curls bounced to her shoulders?

29

Ancy. I could say "Hi Ancy" instead of "Hi there" to prove that I knew it. I tried to picture what she was doing, what a girl did. Her shift at the hardware store must've been over by now, so she'd probably be doing what Leslie was doing downstairs, except Ancy would probably be watching *TRL*.

I'd never been on a date before, so I started making a list of things we could talk about. We'd be eating ice cream, so that was something. We were next to the library and the water, where people from Long Island sailed in to drink at the pier-side bars. We were too young to get served anywhere, but I wondered what she thought of drinking. I had had a few sips of beer when I was little, and I'd hated it. Had she? Did her family drink?

I wondered what she thought of me. Did she think I was smart? Cute? At least passable? I pictured what it would be like to kiss her, and my palms got sweaty.

I'd had one kiss before, at a mixer. The all-boys schools and all-girls schools in the area hosted these dances. Everyone paid five dollars to get in, and the boys from the all-boys school got to meet the girls from the all-girls schools. When the girls' schools hosted, nuns would patrol with rulers, making sure there was room for Jesus. When the boys' schools hosted, the male teachers high-fived the boys.

In the middle of the dance floor whichever school was hosting, there was a pit of people grinding. A human wall sheltering the dancers. When the nuns managed to make it through, they'd break up the grinding, but the dancing never stayed stopped.

It wasn't that I didn't want to grind, too, but that I wasn't sure how it was supposed to work. When the girl put her ass on my dick, was I supposed to get a boner? I knew that I'd want to, but was it allowed? And what if I came in my pants?

Joel wasn't allowed entrance because he didn't go to a private school, but he told me that I was supposed to get wood. That seemed unbelievable. I was supposed to press my erect penis against the butt of a girl I didn't know? Or was it supposed to be soft at the beginning, and she would make it hard?

So instead of dancing, I flowered on the wall, afraid of the fray. At one dance in the gym of my all-boys school, two girls had pointed to me. One led me by the hand out onto the dance floor, and the two grinded on either side of me. At the end of the song, the one in the back yelled, "Kiss him!"

The girl went in for my cheek, but I put my lips in her path. The contact was warm, and lasted for about a quarter of a second before she screamed, "Oh my God."

I was ready to dance for another song, but they were running away laughing, scouting their next nerd.

When my dad picked me up, he asked how it went. I told him that I'd had my first kiss, and he'd asked, "Did you get her phone number?"

"No."

"Mission failed," he'd said, like he was some kind of lady's man.

Things had to go better with Ancy. At the very least, we knew each other's names going in. I wasn't sure about all that advice that Uncle Pauly had given me, but at least I had a strategy. I was going to ask her about the umbrella and then put it up before she could answer like Uncle Pauly said. I didn't know about waiting three days to call her still.

If I kissed her, it would be better. When I kissed her, it was going to be better.

Ancy.

CHAPTER 7

Away Message
Number1AvrilLavigneFanSoComplicated:
Guess who's having a screaming match . . .
again?!
Sam: Fuck you!
Mom: Don't talk like that.
Sam: It's not worth it.

Jeez Louise. Some people are trying to watch
TV!

MOM MADE TACOS for dinner that night. She was, to put it kindly, not culinarily inclined. The recipe came straight off the side of an Old El Paso box with a little seasoning kit and the shells, but it qualified as the big gun in her repertoire. The meal that made all three kids happy and, in some ways, reminded her of her father, who'd probably come over some night when she cooked it, though I can't recall if he ever compared her tacos to the ones he ate growing up in Mexico.

Those seasoning packets were the only hint of spice in our diet. She was so proud that she couldn't help smiling as she brought the plates over.

Uncle Pauly sat in the empty chair on Sam's side of the table. I'd been avoiding seeing or thinking about him, but here he was, sitting across from me, grinning.

Mom put a plate down in front of him.

"Would you mind if we said a short grace, Paul?" For

years, Dad asked every visitor this question, as if they weren't socially obligated to let him pray in his own home.

Everyone bowed their heads and linked hands. Whenever we prayed, I squeezed the shit out of Leslie's hand, trying to get her to cry out. Uncle Pauly being there didn't change that.

"Stop," she whispered.

"Father, thank you for this blessing of food and family that you've bestowed upon us, especially the presence of Ana's wonderful brother, Paul, who will be gracing us with his presence while he gets back up onto his feet."

Dad kept droning on like that for a while. He always did. And then, finally, it was time to eat. Leslie shook her hand away from me. "Jerk."

Normally, I attacked my tacos with vigor. Dad joked that I was like a lawn mower. But tonight, I didn't feel much like eating. I couldn't take my eyes off of Uncle Pauly, the way he lathered salsa and veggies until his tacos overflowed with toppings. I couldn't imagine him using that book. You'd have to be a real bastard to use that kind of thing.

Uncle Pauly said, "Thanks so much for having me," and took a bite out of his taco. My mother was smiling.

Uncle Pauly chewed slowly, then his eyes narrowed. "Ana, where did you get this recipe?"

"It's on the box."

Uncle Pauly had spent the last twenty years opening restaurants in New York City. He smiled. "The box for the toilet paper?"

Sam chortled. Leslie and I laughed. Dad was the only one who managed to keep a straight face.

Mom deflated. "I like it."

"These are the best tacos I've ever tasted," Dad said.

"Then you've got to taste more tacos. Dad's rolling over in his grave and he's not even dead yet," Uncle Pauly said. He laughed at his own joke, but it was catching. Even I broke into a smile.

"I Mexi-can't with these tacos," Sam said, between bites.

"Pass the vegetables, please," Dad said.

"I'll cook tomorrow," Uncle Pauly said. He handed my father a plate with chopped tomatoes and lettuce.

"I'm making chicken Schlemmertopf tomorrow. I already have everything defrosting," Mom said.

"Was that bread I saw thawing? Why did you freeze the bread, Ana?" Uncle Pauly asked.

"When I was in Worcester, the bread would get moldy if I didn't freeze it."

"Didn't you move out of Worcester before you and Dad got married?" Leslie asked.

"It tastes fine once you defrost it," Dad said, trying his damndest to stop the onslaught.

"You're saying if I gave you a slice of bread baked fresh and a slice that was defrosted, they would taste the same?" Uncle Pauly leaned across the table to get a better look at Dad.

"Drop it, Pauly," Mom said, her posture imploding.

"Okay, okay. I'm a guest. I'm glad you're teaching your kids our heritage. I feel like I'm in Mexico City." He waved a taco to emphasize his point.

"We have piñatas for the birthdays, too," Mom said.

"And we dressed as Mexicans for Halloween one year," I said, barely able to hold back a giggle. It baffled me. If we were Mexican—and Grandpa certainly had emigrated from Mexico—why were we drawing on fake mustaches and wearing sombreros for Halloween?

Mom sighed. She looked like a boxer who'd been beaten badly in the last round.

"The Party City piñatas preserve our heritage," Uncle Pauly said.

"Does anyone have anything else they want to talk about?" Dad said. He was rubbing his temples now, tacos forgotten on his plate in front of him.

"I'm going to GameStop and buying *Grand Theft Auto: Vice City*," Sam announced.

SAY UNCLE

"Can I watch?" Leslie asked.

"Of course. We're going to spend a nice family evening watching Sam kill prostitutes to get his money back," Uncle Pauly said.

I wouldn't have guessed that Uncle Pauly knew about that. Maybe Paul Jr. had the game.

Watching Uncle Pauly call out my parents on the little hypocrisies in the bedrock of the family, things I saw but couldn't say, was exhilarating. It was like seeing a rated-R movie for the first time.

Mom was in shambles over her plate. Looking back on it, I feel like a real piece of shit. The kind of bastard who would use that damn book. Sure, Mom's food didn't live up to the standards of Uncle Pauly, who'd worked in restaurants for twenty years. I can't hit a baseball as hard as a major leaguer, either. I should've told him to shut up, should've sided with Mom and Dad no matter how much fun we had laughing at them. I should've done a lot of things.

CHAPTER 8

Away Message
FancyAncy89: BRB having the best day ever
:). Nobody tell my mom ROFL!

IT TOOK ME an hour to choose what to wear. I asked Leslie for help, adding in a whisper, "It's for a date."

"Because I'm a girl?" Leslie asked, confused.

I blushed.

"Let's look at her MySpace," she said, and we went downstairs.

I should've thought of that myself. 2005 was a transitional period for the internet. I still mainly used AIM, but even then, I barely logged on. Leslie was three years younger and had lied about being thirteen to get on MySpace.

We found Ancy quickly. "Livin' la Vida Loca" played as we entered her page. Her profile picture featured her in comically oversized New York Giants shoulder pads.

"Should I wear my Giants jersey?" I asked. The jersey in question was a children's large Jeremy Shockey that accentuated the small bumps of my biceps.

"Too obvious," Leslie said. "Anyway, you don't know if she likes the Giants or she just thought it was a cute photo."

I nodded. The struggle with getting dressed originated from the fact that Mom bought my clothes and we had different mental images of who I was as a person. I saw myself as a rockstar-in-training. She saw me as someone ready to step onto a sailboat at any time.

SAY UNCLE

Half of Ancy's Top 8 were Indian folks I didn't know, rounded out by some girls I vaguely remembered from middle school. One was obsessed with musical theater and the other barely spoke. I guessed Ancy still hung out with them.

"Click on her pictures," I said.

"You know what she looks like already. You want to see what kind of stuff she says," Leslie said. Even my eleven year old sister knew more than I did.

Ancy had posted a lot of song lyrics. She loved the bridge of "Livin' la Vida Loca," which played the entire time we stalked her page. More surprising, though, was how often she posted dad jokes. One really got me:

Knock knock.
Who's there?
Let us.
'Let us' who?
Let us in. It's cold outside!

It shouldn't have been that funny, but I was so damn happy to have a date.

We would've kept looking, but Sam bounded down the stairs and said, "What are you looking at?"

"Neopets," Leslie said and exed out of MySpace.

We didn't get a clue what to wear, but Leslie said, "Just be you."

To me that meant a Led Zeppelin with the naked angel t-shirt paired with cargo shorts that would've fit a man double my size. Leslie added an Abercrombie button down, open with the sleeves rolled up to complete the look.

I was worried about what Ancy would think and Uncle Pauly gave me a lot of time to stew on it when I went downstairs. "Don't worry. You're going to be fashionably late," he said.

I nodded, then said what I really thought. "Wouldn't it be better if I were fashionably on time?"

He shook his head. "You don't get it. You're nervous, right?"

"No."

"Don't try to be cool with me. Save it for the chick. You feel how nervous you are?"

God, I did. "Yes."

"She's feeling that nervous too."

"So shouldn't I be there on time?"

"No. We're going to use it. She waits, she's feeling nervous. She's obsessing about you, whether you're actually going to show up or not. Then, guess what? You come walking down the street and she can't stop smiling. She likes you, so of course she's smiling, but she's smiling more because she wasn't sure if you were going to be there. See?"

"Isn't that . . . " I tried to think of the right word. Manipulative? Cruel? Shitty?

"Do you want her to like you or not?"

"I do, but I don't want to hurt her."

"Listen, Braden, men and women aren't meant to be together. Women are crazy. Your Aunt Linda is spazzing out so bad that I had to come here. But in a month, she's going to be begging me to come home and when she does, I'm going to make her wait. She's been calling every day, and I let it ring straight through to voicemail. That's the definition of insanity. Every time she calls, she expects me to pick up. You gotta play with their crazy."

I should've said no, but I nodded. I thought about that book, and if anything he was saying now was in it.

"Because you're dealing with a crazy person, you have to play into their neuroses. Maybe you're going to lose your virginity this summer."

I froze, blushing. I'd been wondering about what a real kiss would feel like. If Ancy's breath would be minty.

"Now you're listening. Let's go."

SAY UNCLE

Uncle Pauly dropped me two blocks from the hardware store so I could walk over. Ancy stood waiting in front of the store, wearing her red uniform vest, looking back and forth. Her hands were clamped tight. I saw her for real this time, not the girl she was in the fantasies I'd concocted.

She was tall and thin, wearing form fitting jeans and a low-cut pink shirt. Her jaw was set tight, and then she saw me. Her features loosened into a smile. She waved, as though I weren't looking right at her. She almost hopped. I waved back.

She started walking toward me. I walked faster, struggling not to jog. In my head, Uncle Pauly's voice told me not to be too eager.

"Hey," I said. She didn't have much, but I had to resist staring at her cleavage.

I waved as she went in for a hug. She backed up and I went for a hug as she waved. Then, we got on the same page, and we wrapped our arms around each other's shoulders, with a little room for Jesus downstairs.

"How are you?" she asked.

"Good, Ancy," I said, jamming her name into the conversation. "How are you?"

"I'm nervous." She laughed. "I don't know if I should tell you that, but I am."

Uncle Pauly's advice flew out of my head. "Me too."

We both laughed. We stood in front of her work, taking each other in for a minute.

"We better get to the ice cream. How long is your break?"

"Oh, I'm not working today." She took off the vest. "My parents wouldn't want me to be doing this. Not with a boy."

"You snuck out?" I asked, leaving off, *to see me*.

"I don't lie to my parents a lot." She'd told them she had to be in at 9, but walked to the library for the morning. They were going to pick her up in front of the hardware store in an hour.

"Do you want to walk?" I asked.

39

Together the two of us made our way toward Scoopy Doo's. The downtown was small, a green surrounded by shops leading from the train station down to the harbor.

"I've got a joke for you," she said.

"Oh yeah?"

"How do you make an octopus laugh?"

"How?"

"Ten-tickles." She laughed at her own joke. I tried not to join her, but it was contagious.

Once I caught my breath, I asked, "Why don't your parents want you to date?"

I hadn't told my parents, either, but it wouldn't surprise me if Uncle Pauly had. I really didn't want Sam to know. In first grade, I'd had a crush on Kim Clink and Sam had sung about how I was in love with her until I cried.

"They want an arranged marriage for me."

"Oh," I said. I had a vague notion of what that entailed from *The Simpsons*.

"I'm not going to get one." She brushed my bicep with the palm of her hand, as though she were holding me up. I loved it. She was so gentle.

"Me neither."

We both laughed. We waited for the light at a crosswalk. Downtown was near empty on a weekday afternoon. A few people bustled about on their lunch breaks, not relaxed like us.

"You're at Precious Blood now, right? The all-boys school?" she asked.

"Yeah." I braced myself. Usually when another guy found out about the kind of school I went to, they cracked a gay joke. Girls, on the other hand, were still a mystery to me.

The light turned and we walked across the street. "I wish I could go to an all-girls school."

"Why?" I asked, nearly yelling. Who would want that?

"When you're a girl, guys look at you all the time. I'm trying to focus. I want to be a lawyer, so I need to do well on my SATs so I can get into a good college."

"Because of your parents?" I asked.

"No. My dad says I would be a good teacher."

I nodded. "But why a lawyer? I heard the Bar is like impossible."

"I want to work with immigrants. I saw everything my parents went through coming here, and it wasn't fair. They're smart, hard working people and, sorry, I'm going off. What do you want to be?"

"A rock star."

"Oh," she said, glancing at the Led Zeppelin design on my shirt. "That's why you're wearing a naked man on your chest."

I blushed, and grabbed around for something to say.

"It's okay. I'm joking with you. What instrument do you play?"

"None, yet. I'm going to take the guitar class in school this fall. My parents got me into it so I'll keep going to Precious Blood."

We arrived at the ice cream shop. There was no line, but we stayed back from the clerk while Ancy read over the flavors.

"What are you going to get?" she asked.

"What I get every time. Rocky Road."

"I think I'll take a scoop of Moose Tracks and a scoop of sea salt caramel on a waffle cone."

"You got it," I said.

Before I could order, Ancy said, "Make that raspberry dark chocolate and coffee in a cup."

"Okay," I said. I took a slow step forward. "You're sure, this time?"

"Yes. Sea salt caramel and raspberry dark chocolate on a sugar cone."

I ordered before she could change her mind again. Outside, all of the tables were open, so we took the one closest to the water. The little channel was full of motor boats that seated four.

Conversation really took off at the table. She told me

what the kids from our middle school were like. Brandon Rote had been expelled the first day of high school for bringing a hunting knife. Ryan Greenway was still getting bullied. There was a rumor that Amanda Smith was pregnant and Brandon Rote was the father. Seventh grade legend had it that they'd fucked in a closet during detention.

I told her more about what it was like at the all-boys school. There was no one to dress up for, so guys would leave the uniform white button-down shirt and tie in their locker every day after school for months straight. When we hit each other in the halls, one English teacher would walk down the hall and yell, "Good one," with his lisp. Mr. Pallino taught a one-day-a-week class called "Life Choices" instead of sex ed and he TALKED LIKE THIS with his *speech* VARYING volumes to keep your attention. We didn't talk about condoms, but we did watch *St. Elmo's Fire*.

She couldn't believe it. I forgot all about Uncle Pauly's umbrella trick. I felt so warm. I could do this forever, sit at this table across from Ancy and listen to her tell me about her family, her life.

"I like you," she said.

It was a non-sequitur, but one that made me happy. Her ice cream had started melting. A line of raspberry dark chocolate dribbled down her hand before she dabbed it with a napkin. Mine was long gone, and I was regretting not offering her a bite.

"I like you too," I said. I edged in a little. "Should we kiss?"

"Should we?" She smiled. "Do you think you can?"

I leaned in slowly. Uncle Pauly had given a lot of advice on how to play games to get to this moment. I didn't know how far I should go in, how much to open my lips, how to angle my head.

She met me halfway. The kiss was quick, a peck really, but it sent a supernova of endorphins shooting through me.

SAY UNCLE

She pulled back while I sat there, halfway across the table.

"Was that good?" I asked, as I finally resettled into my chair.

Her knee grazed mine under the table. "It was great."

"Can I get your number?" I said.

She took out a piece of paper from her purse with her home phone on it.

"But don't call until after ten. Both of my parents work the night shift. If a boy calls . . . " She rolled her eyes to the back of her head and dragged her thumb across her throat.

For a second, I pictured the diagram of the woman in my uncle's book. I blinked it away.

"For both of us. Not just me," Ancy said.

"I can manage that." Who else was going to need the phone that late?

"Should we kiss again?" she asked.

"One more for the road."

We were more confident this time. It was heaven. Against Uncle Pauly's advice, we made plans for another date two days later.

CHAPTER 9

Away Message
BrayDay327: Thinking about you ;)

AFTER MY DATE, I walked up to Joel's with my *Penthouse* stuffed under my shirt. The corner jabbed into my pec, near the nipple. I kept adjusting my shirt, trying to keep the sweat off the cover.

As I climbed the stoop, Joel yelled, "Mom, Braden is here with his porno magazine."

"Braden has a porno magazine?" she yelled back.

"It's his first one. He's going to hide it here."

"Why do you need to tell me?" she screamed.

Joel opened the door. "Oh, did you hear that?"

"Shut up." I pulled the *Penthouse* out from under my shirt.

"How did the date go?" We walked up to his room. I sat on the side of his bed.

"It was amazing. Her name is Ancy. Your grandpa was dead-on with the yearbook."

"Did she suck your dick?"

I laughed. "Yeah, right out there on the green with everyone watching. Then again on the steps of city hall. The mayor gave me the key to the city after."

"It's a national holiday."

"Mayors can't make national holidays, numb nuts. They're only in charge of the city."

"That's the private school talking." He put some weed in his grinder.

44

SAY UNCLE

"The mayor's an alum."

"Of course he is."

"Didn't your school have the world's fattest cow or something?" I didn't give him a chance to answer, "Sorry. I was thinking of your mom."

"Oh, Braden's got jokes. You want me to call her in here so she can hear you say that?"

"Truce, truce."

He emptied the grinder onto rolling paper.

"I saw something weird in my uncle's desk," I said.

"Other than your first porno mag?"

"Yeah. Yeah. It was this creepy book. I touched it by accident, and it felt strange. The binding was all crumbly."

"An old book?" He licked the edge of the paper and rolled it into a joint.

"There were these pictures inside."

"A really old porno book?"

"No, man. It was a diagram of how to rip out a person's heart."

Joel stopped patting down the edges of his joint. "What the fuck."

"I saw something weird in his room in New York, too."

"This is the Uncle Pauly who got you the date?"

"Yeah."

"That solves it then. He's giving you one last happy month before he sacrifices you." Joel cherried the joint, then held it out for me.

I declined. I'd tried it once in eighth grade and Joel convinced me that someone was making a reality TV show of my life like in *The Truman Show*. "There was a dark room in his apartment that smelled mossy, like his book. And he had the knife from the picture."

"Dude, listen to me. You're mincemeat."

"The book was written in this weird language too. It wasn't Latin, Russian, Spanish, English."

"Chinese or Japanese?"

"No."

Joel took a puff, then hacked up a lung. After recovering, he asked, "Did you take a picture?"

"With what?"

"Dude, you've got to get a phone. What about your dad's camera?"

"What would we even do with a picture?"

Uncle Pauly kept the door lock's key in his pocket, and even if I could get it, he would know it was missing as soon as he got back to my room. So I had to wait for my moment. In the meantime, I hadn't made Ancy wait three days. I snuck the phone upstairs to Sam's room while he played *Age of Empires II* on the desktop that same night, shortly after ten.

The phone rang twice before she picked up. Nervous pressure nearly caved in my chest. I imagined the caller ID at her house, shouting out "O'Riley, Michael" in its robotic voice.

"Hi. Is Ancy there?"

"Braden?" she said, voice hushed.

"It's after ten. Like you said." I paced Sam's room, trying to burn off some of the anxious energy.

"Just wait a second," she said, voice hushed.

"Sure." I pictured what she'd be wearing at home, out of her work uniform. She'd been into flower-print clothing in middle school, so I pictured her in a shirt covered in sunflowers.

"Okay," she said, voice regular volume now. "I'm in the garage. My cousin's watching TV in the other room, so I'm good until my dad comes home at midnight."

I realized I was grinning stupidly despite the nerves. Talking to her felt like eating a cinnamon roll. There was an awkward pause.

"I liked eating ice cream with you," she said.

"I liked eating ice cream with you too," I said.

SAY UNCLE

And we kept going like that, talking about nothing. Blue was both of our favorite colors, me because of the New York Giants and her for no particular reason. My favorite show was *The Simpsons*. No surprise, hers was *Law and Order*, but she also loved *Friends*, which I refrained from saying I didn't get. All of the stuff about Uncle Pauly and his book melted and sloshed out of my head while I was talking to Ancy, all that dread replaced—or maybe just covered—by butterflies.

That was what was happening when Sam barged in without knocking. "Who are you talking to? And why is your voice high like that?"

I turned red. I tried to keep my cool, knowing that getting into another fight with Sam wouldn't make it any better. Ancy would think I was from a family of psychopaths.

"Who's that?" Ancy asked.

Sam ran downstairs. I was too embarrassed to chase him. The other line clicked on. "Does Bray Bray have a girlfriend?" he sing-songed.

"Get off the phone, Sam," I yelled.

But of course he didn't. "What's your name, Braden's girlfriend?"

"I'm not anybody's girlfriend," Ancy said, which somehow made me feel worse than anything Sam could have said.

"Sam, get off the phone, please," I said.

"Or what?" Sam asked. He hummed a tune and even without words I knew it was, *Braden's got a girlfriend, Braden's got a girlfriend.*

"I'm going to go," Ancy said. "Let you two work out whatever this is."

"No. Sam's getting off the phone—right, Sam?"

"Nope. I'm going to get to know your girlfriend."

The dial tone droned. "You asshole," I yelled as I ran down the stairs.

"Braden's got a girlfriend," he sang.

Mom, Dad, and Leslie were at the table playing Life, laughing.

"You fucking asshole. Why do you have to be such a dick all the time?"

"Language," Dad said.

"What're you going to do about it?" Sam said. He stood from the computer in the corner of the room. He'd gone to the gym every day for the last two years. I went with him enough to know exactly how much stronger than me he was.

"I'm going to kick your ass," I said.

"Braden, stop," Mom said.

A hand grabbed my shoulder. Uncle Pauly had come up behind me. "What's going on?"

"Sam ruined my phone call with Ancy," I said. Uncle Pauly's hand clamped me in place.

"And now Braden's going to cry," Sam said, and wiped away imaginary tears.

"Where's your girlfriend, Sam?" Uncle Pauly asked.

Silence punctured the room. Normally, Sam would've taken these as fighting words, but Uncle Pauly was a mammoth of a man.

"Pauly, don't talk to him like that," Mom said.

"Do you hear him talking to Braden? Seventeen-year-old virgin is making fun of the fifteen-year-old for having a date and you're sitting here laughing. "

"Sam is just blowing off a little steam. He's been studying for the SATs all day," Dad said.

"You got three kids," Uncle Pauly said. "You got to raise 'em all."

"Fuck you, Pauly," Sam said.

Uncle Pauly let go of my shoulder and took a step toward Sam. "Oh yeah?"

Sam quivered. He looked stuck, fists balled like he wanted to throw a punch, lip quivering like he wanted to cry.

"That's what I thought. Stop messing with your

brother. He's got a girl and you don't. Stop being such a little brat and I'll help you meet a girl, too."

"Who was your date with?" Mom asked.

"Oh, no," I said.

Uncle Pauly slapped me on the back and I knew it was going to have to come out.

"Her name is Ancy. She works at the hardware store." I blushed.

"What does she look like?" Leslie asked.

"Oh, she's gorgeous. You might not meet her for a while, but when you do, trust me, you're going to be blown away," Uncle Pauly said.

"She told me she's not Braden's girlfriend," Sam said, still sulking in the corner.

CHAPTER 10

Away Message
EnterSamMan88: FUCK EVERYTHING!!! FUCK
EVERYONE!!! I'LL GET YOU BACK!!!

JOEL'S GRANDFATHER INADVERTENTLY modeled the solution to getting past Uncle Pauly's locked door. With Fox News blaring on the TV, he took a handle of vodka to the face and passed out. Or as they called it in Joel's house, Tuesday. I needed to get Uncle Pauly drunk and keep him downstairs until he went comatose.

I could wait out everyone else no problem. I'd been staying up late since the start of the summer, putting on *The Late Show*, then *The Late Late Show*, until Conan came on. The shows were fine, funny even. But really, I wanted to be able to masturbate without having to worry about anyone walking in on me. The only room in the house with a lock was the bathroom, and Sam had figured out how to wiggle the doorknob so it popped open ten years ago. At least all this practice meant out-waiting Uncle Pauly would be a cakewalk.

Life would be so much easier if I had a car and a license, but I was going to need my dad's help to carry out this plan. I found him in the master bathroom, with the faceplate taken off the light switch.

"Hey, Dad. Can you take me to Blockbuster when you're done with that?"

"Come over here and look at this, Braden."

SAY UNCLE

There was a metal frame screwed into the wall with wires snaking back toward the wood behind it.

"The light has been taking a second to turn on, so I'm adjusting," he said.

"Adjusting" was code for "fucking around." The house wasn't falling apart, but there was plenty wrong with it. He worked late most nights, but once every few Saturdays he would pretend to be handy. Some projects, like my closet door that had fallen out of the runner when we'd first moved in ten years ago, fell onto the backburner. Others he would start, taking apart whatever wasn't working and then neglect to put it back together. Once in a blue moon, he'd crush it, fixing whatever and making it look easy. We never knew which it would be.

He held up a red wire. "This is the one that's not working, so I tightened the connection. Run to the basement and flip the fuse back on."

"And then we'll go to Blockbuster?" I asked.

"One day you're going to have your own house. Don't you want to know how to fix it?"

"I'm going to pay someone to do it."

"I didn't know you were going to be rich. When you figure out the secret, tell me. Until then, go flip the fuse."

"And then we'll go?"

"Fine, yes. Once this is finished."

So I went down and flipped the fuse. A second later, he howled. The light wasn't fixed and he'd gotten shocked, but a deal was a deal.

Back then, I tried to convince someone to take me to Blockbuster every weekend. I adored movies, in large part because the women in films were the only ones I saw and I stuck to the genres where they might take their shirts off: horror and comedy. But that wasn't necessarily what Uncle Pauly would watch. I didn't know whether or not he even liked movies. But I knew what he liked to watch on Sunday afternoons, so I grabbed a shotgun spread of football

51

movies: *Remember the Titans*, *Friday Night Lights*, and *The Longest Yard*.

"When did you get so into football?" my dad asked as we waited in line next to a shelf of new releases. Customers stretched halfway across the store on a Saturday night.

"I want something Uncle Pauly will like."

"That's really sweet of you." There was something wistful in the way he said it, like he wanted to know why I never rented movies he might like. "There's something we need to talk about with your uncle."

We stepped forward mechanically, moving past a display of magazines with pictures of celebrities and stopping in front of another filled with microwave popcorn.

"You don't want to be like him. I mean, the way he's ignoring Aunt Linda's calls, it's not right." When there was a crowd, Dad performed, but he got preachy when he caught you one on one.

"I know."

"He treats relationships like a game." We moved past the popcorn to a shelf of toys.

A little girl in front of us picked up a princess in a blister package and held it up for her mother. The mother waved it away.

"I don't want you to be like that," he said.

"I'm not." The way Dad wasn't listening to me pissed me off. At fifteen, I was constantly angry with him, but when he tried to get serious I lost it.

"I know, I know. You think you know everything now. But you've got to try to understand—"

"Shut up," I said.

I turned away from him. A middle-aged man holding the three Terminator movies shot me a dirty look.

"If you want to watch these movies, you better not talk to me like that," Dad said. He stepped forward. We were next in line. I wasn't going to mess this up.

"Sorry, Dad," I said, trying not to sound flippant but failing miserably.

SAY UNCLE

"All I'm saying is to think about what your uncle does. He's your mother's brother and he loves you. He wants the best for you, but sometimes the way he does things, it's not good for other people."

Phase 1 involved casually mentioning to Uncle Pauly that my dad had some nice whiskey stashed away in the laundry room for special occasions. To Dad, that meant holidays, birthdays, and weddings. For Uncle Pauly, it meant now was a fine time to get plastered.

Phase 2 was showing Uncle Pauly what we rented. He couldn't wait to rewatch *Remember the Titans*, or to see *Friday Night Lights* for the first time. He was quick to remind anyone who would listen that he'd given a knee to football when he was nineteen, a sacrifice that he'd make again if things would have only turned out a little bit differently.

What I didn't expect was that everyone else would want to watch *Remember the Titans,* too. The adults squeezed onto the couch with a big bowl of microwave popcorn. Sam rolled over the computer chair and put his feet up on the back of the couch, while Leslie and I were consigned to sprawling out on the floor.

The popcorn got passed around and the whiskey went back and forth between my father and Uncle Pauly. At one point, Uncle Pauly asked if Sam could have a drink, to which my parents replied, "No," in unison.

Mom conked off in the first half hour of the movie. Not a surprise. Dad made it a little longer. They went to bed and I stole their spot on the couch.

Sam grabbed a Dixie cup and Uncle Pauly poured him some whiskey. I wasn't expecting Sam to have brought another one for me.

"Can I have some?" Leslie asked.

"Absolutely not. Whiskey puts hair on your chest," Uncle Pauly said.

She turned back to the movie, where they were singing "Ain't No Mountain High Enough" and dancing in the locker room.

I could smell the alcohol from an arm's length away. I didn't want to drink it.

"This is our summer, guys. We're going to meet so many girls. You're going to be drowning in it."

I stifled myself from asking what about Aunt Linda. Uncle Pauly held up his glass. Sam and I cheersed with our Dixie cups. Sam drank his right down. His eyes bulged. Then he coughed.

Uncle Pauly laughed. "It's sipping whiskey. Don't shoot it."

I didn't do anything with mine.

"Can I have another?" Sam asked.

"Let Braden drink his first," Uncle Pauly said.

"Why don't you take mine, Sam?" I said.

Uncle Pauly blocked my attempt to pass the Dixie cup to Sam. "Nah. Either we're all-in or we're putting the whiskey away."

"Shhh, I can't hear," Leslie said.

My hand was shaking, slightly. I coached myself into bringing the cup to my lips. The smell seared my nostrils. I took another second before tossing it back. It burned, then I was coughing too.

"What did I just tell your brother? It's for sipping," Uncle Pauly said.

Leslie took the remote and jacked up the TV volume. We weren't supposed to fill the bar past the "L" in "VOLUME" but she had it around the "E" now.

"You still want another?" Uncle Pauly asked us.

"Yes," Sam said.

"Braden?"

I had to get rid of Sam, somehow. "Yes."

I really sipped the next one, like Uncle Pauly said. The liquor chapped my lips. Sam kept shooting them, though.

I felt it in my head first, warm and fuzzy. I got why they

called it a "buzz." Sam kept doing them as shots, and then he was running up the stairs with his hand over his mouth.

If Uncle Pauly were a responsible adult, he probably would have gone with him, but he didn't. That left me, him, and Leslie. And she took care of herself. When the movie ended, she didn't want to watch *Friday Night Lights*, and that was the one Uncle Pauly had wanted to see.

"You want some more whiskey?" he asked as the movie opened.

"I don't want to end up like Sam."

He laughed. "In more ways than one, Braden."

I tracked the twenty minutes it took for Uncle Pauly's eyes to close on the faceplate of the DVD player and then waited another five. His head tipped back, and he started to gently snore. I leaned in close. The whiskey soured his breath. I whispered, "Pauly," once. He didn't move. Then I said it louder. Nothing.

Gently, I reached into his pocket, trying not to touch his leg. I wrapped a finger around his keyring. It had absorbed his warmth. I pulled, but they were stuffed in tight.

His head was still back, the snores rumbling past the popcorn kernels stuck in his teeth on their way out of his mouth now. My finger hooked the keyring. What did he need these for, anyway? A housekey, a key for his apartment, and one for my room were all I had anticipated, but he had five or ten more jamming up the works.

I tugged, harder this time. The keys budged. Uncle Pauly's snores stopped. His eyes twitched. I froze, holding my breath. On the TV, pads slapped against pads as someone got leveled. A crowd went wild. Uncle Pauly coughed once, then the snoring resumed.

The third time, the keys came out. Uncle Pauly didn't seem to react. I didn't know how long that would last, so I grabbed the family Nikon from the coffee table in the living room. I'd cleared some space on an old SIM card earlier, deleting the outtakes from Christmases and first Holy Communions.

On my way upstairs, I was fiddling with the camera settings and didn't notice Sam until nearly bumping into him at the top of the stairs.

"What are you doing?" he asked, pale and shivering.

"I'm going to the bathroom."

"Oh, no you're not," he said, and ran for the door.

So I had until he was done puking to find the right key. I ruled out the biggest keys, the smallest ones, and our house key right off, which left three to try. The bathroom was straight across the hall from my room. Sam was running the faucet to cover the sounds of his vomiting. I kept an eye on that door as I shoved keys in the new lock. One clicked in. I nearly fell through the door. I swung it shut as Sam emerged from the bathroom and staggered out into the hallway. He padded closer. His door was next to mine, so I couldn't be sure where he was going.

He bumped into my door. It rattled in its frame. "I need a ginger ale," he said, though I'm not sure to whom. Then the knob of his door turned. His footsteps got quieter until I heard him collapse onto the bed.

Thank God. I turned on the light and grabbed the book. It opened to the picture with the diagram again and I snapped some pictures. I flipped the pages, taking some more. I wanted enough photos that we'd have something to reference when we posted it online.

Heavy footsteps plodded up the stairs. I jammed the book back into the desk and climbed into the closet and stood behind the only standing door. Uncle Pauly creaked up the next set of steps and paused in front of the door as I waited for it to open. I'd forgotten to turn the light off. He was going to catch me again. But the door didn't open. He mumbled something about the goddamn keys and then headed back down.

I hit the light, slipped out of my room, closed the door quietly as I could, and then stashed the camera under the sink in the bathroom. I flushed the toilet and washed my hands as loud as I could before I headed back downstairs.

SAY UNCLE

Uncle Pauly was down there. He'd stopped the movie and turned on the light. The whiskey bottle was near empty on the side table next to the popcorn bowl with only kernels left.

"Where'd you go, Braden?"

"To the bathroom," I said, needing him to believe me.

"Why didn't you pause the movie?"

"I thought you were still watching it."

"I was asleep."

"Really? I asked you if I should turn it off and you said, 'No.'"

"Huh." He looked around the room. "Have you seen my keys?"

"Have you checked under the couch cushions?"

"Yeah, as a matter of fact. I have."

"What about in the bowl, where Mom puts keys she finds?"

"No." He squinted at me, and then went to the bowl. When he looked down to sort through the five sets of keys, I stuffed his actual set in between the cushions.

"You really checked in the couch?"

"Yeah. I really did."

"But they're in there now." I lifted the cushion and pointed so he would have to come over and find them himself.

He moved slowly, interrogating me with his eyes. I held myself like an innocent person would, but I didn't know where to put my arms. At my sides? In my pockets? At least I knew to keep my face still as a statue.

Uncle Pauly snatched his keys from the couch cushion. "All right." His voice was as paranoid as his eyes. "I'm going to bed."

CHAPTER 11

Away Message
bigRican787: Anybody know anything about magic books? Not the reading kind. Asking for a friend.

I DIDN'T HAVE much time to worry about it, because my next date with Ancy was that morning. My parents had already agreed to take Leslie to the mall. Sam had his license, but I knew better than to ask him. So it was down to Uncle Pauly.

He was typing something on the family desktop. I was slouching, even though I knew I shouldn't be. Uncle Pauly would've told me himself, it all comes down to confidence.

"Could you give me a ride please?" I asked.

"Where?" he said without looking up.

"Subway." When he didn't reply, I added, "With Ancy."

"The practice girl? You weren't even supposed to call her yet." The lenses of his reading glasses magnified his pupils when he turned toward me.

"She said we should go for dinner since we already had dessert. Then the next date, we're going to have appetizers."

"That's cute." He took off the glasses. "You let her have all that power right off the bat?"

Maybe I should've asked Sam.

"I'll drive you, but it's a bad idea. If you've got her number, just call her and tell her something came up. If you can make it sound like a date with someone else without saying that . . . "

"I think I'll go on my date."

Uncle Pauly shrugged. "Suit yourself."

Uncle Pauly grabbed Dad's keys and we were off. We backed out of the driveway and headed toward Route 1. "Braden, I need to ask you. What is it that you're looking for?"

"With Ancy?" I asked, even though I knew what he meant.

"I've caught you snooping, twice. You know if you want something, it's your room. But I'm asking that you respect my privacy."

"I needed to see my yearbook. And I didn't want anyone to know about my *Penthouse*."

He evaluated me, eyes off the road. We were heading for a yellow light.

"Uncle Pauly."

Instead of gunning it to make it through, he jerked the car to a stop. My head bounced against the seat. We were just two minutes away from downtown.

"Is there something you saw in there? Maybe you didn't mean to, but something sparked your interest."

The heat was rising in my cheeks even as I tried to push it down. "No. No. Nope. I didn't see anything."

The light turned green. We eased out.

Uncle Pauly nodded slowly. "If you did see something, I'd much rather have you come to me to talk about it. The same way if I'd found your porno mag, I would talk to you first, not your parents."

"I really appreciate you, not mentioning that to them." I fidgeted. Seat belts didn't normally bother me, but I was acutely aware of the one I was wearing.

"If I'm going to cover for you, I need to know what you keep coming into my room for. Because you got your porno mag and your yearbook, but we both know something funky happened with my keys last night."

"You were drinking—"

"I checked in between the cushions. Nothing. You

check between the cushions, boom. Keys. I might've thought it was the whiskey, but I went upstairs and the door was already unlocked. I wasn't drinking when I came down."

The car pulled up outside the Subway, kitty-corner from the hardware store.

"You could've forgotten to lock it. And maybe the keys were hanging off something, and they fell when I moved them. Anyway, I can get out here." I grabbed the door handle, but Uncle Pauly had turned the child lock on.

"No. I've been thinking about it all morning. I think I know what you saw, even if you don't want to say it. I want you to know, if you saw what I think you saw, that everything I'm doing is for this family. You understand?"

Uncle Pauly stared at me, his emotions masked. I didn't know if he was threatening me or making me a deal.

Ancy had snagged the high-top table in the corner. "Sorry, I ordered. My break's only half an hour," she said. She held up half of a sub toward me, a meatball precariously close to plopping out of the bread. Normally I'd eat a whole footlong by myself, but I took it.

She slid her drink to the middle of the table.

I sipped through her straw. I hated the chemical taste of Diet Coke, but I said, "Thanks," and tried to smile. Uncle Pauly was still in my head.

"So how are you?"

For a second I thought about telling her what was going on with Uncle Pauly's book, then I thought how stupid would it be for me to admit that I was sneaking into my own bedroom for a porno magazine. So I said, "Good. How are you?"

"I'm good."

There was an awkward pause. Damn Uncle Pauly.

"How's work going?" This time I forced a smile.

SAY UNCLE

"You're weird."

"Ouch." I put down my half of the sub, not a bite out of it.

"I mean today. You're different than how you were last time."

"Some strange stuff is going on at my house."

The silence stretched before she asked, "Like what?"

"My uncle Pauly moved into my room, so I'm sleeping on my brother's floor."

"Don't you hate that? I had my own room for like six months and then my uncle came from India and my cousins got my room. Remember Augustine?"

"Yeah. He didn't speak English when he came to our middle school, so me and my friend Joel taught him swear words. When the teachers yelled at him, he pointed at us and we pretended like we had never talked to him before." I waited for Ancy to laugh. I was a stupid kid.

The air went stale between us. She crossed her arms over her hardware store apron. "He's my cousin."

"I didn't know," I said, even though she had just said that. Oh, shit. "I'm sorry."

"He got my room and I had to move in with my brother. He's eight years older, and he's still learning English, too." Ancy sounded far away now.

"What language do they all speak?" I asked. Maybe I should've apologized again instead.

"Malayalam."

"Can I hear it?"

"No. That's rude." She took the soda to her side of the table from the middle.

"I'm sorry," I said. I didn't see what was rude about it, but I wasn't digging my hole any deeper.

"I don't talk on command. I'm not a dog."

"I didn't think of it that way."

"It's fine." Some marinara sauce fell off her sandwich onto her hand. "Would you get me a napkin?"

"Of course," I said, and went to the napkin holder over

the trash can feeling like an idiot. Why had I told her about Augustine? I had blown it. And I hadn't done any of Uncle Pauly's tricks. What an idiot.

I gave her the napkin and she wiped off her hand. "People ask me worse questions, all the time."

She looked more tired than mad.

"People come up to me and start talking Hindi or Punjabi. I'm Indian, but I don't speak those."

"That sucks," I said.

"And then one year I went to get this photo with Santa Claus and instead of saying cheese, Santa said, 'Say Namaste.'" She laughed a little bit, but it was bitter.

"I'm part Mexican," I volunteered, as if it would exonerate me.

She squinted at me.

"My grandfather immigrated in the sixties. He married a white lady, and their daughter married a white guy, so I look like this." I held up my arm to show how pale it was.

"Do you speak Spanish? At home?"

"Solo un poco," I said, the creme de la freshman class.

She laughed and fired back a Spanish sentence so fast that it made my head spin.

"No. I guess I don't speak Spanish."

"I think I need to go back to work," she said. I looked around for a clock but didn't find one. It couldn't have been more than fifteen minutes.

"Are you sure?"

"Yes," she said. "I'm sure about a lot of things."

Ancy left without scheduling a third date. This time we didn't kiss.

CHAPTER 12

Away Message
FancyAncy89: Love finding out guys I have a crush on bullied my cousin. Super great. Would recommend it to everyone.

AFTER I GOT HOME, I collected the memory card and headed for Joel's, feeling like absolute shit. I thought about how easy it would've been not to tell her we'd taught Augustine curse words. Why did I think she would laugh at that?

There was a vacant lot in between my house and his, cordoned off on either side by bushes. In the winter, we'd hide in them to throw snowballs at passing cars. I should've seen it coming.

I heard some rustling. I froze. A light breeze jostled the shrubs. "Joel?"

No one answered.

I wondered if this was what the drivers felt like when we pelted them. It could've been a rabbit, a squirrel falling down. Nothing that concerned me.

Sam ran out of the bushes. He was bigger, maybe six inches taller and thirty pounds of muscle heavier.

The wind was leaving my lungs before I processed him running at me. I coughed. Being thrown didn't hurt so much until I landed on the grass of the vacant lot. My organs bounced around. My jaw clacked shut. I blinked twice and Sam's knees were on my elbows.

"You think you're such hot shit," he said.

I tried to figure out what he was talking about. Anger is like rain in my family, it comes whether you expect it or not. The men, me included, are the type to let their anger build without a word, pushing closer and closer to the edge. Then, without a sign, they fall over the cliff.

"Laughing at me," he said. His eyes were stung red with badly covered up tears. "Did you put Uncle Pauly up to it?"

"No."

"Why is he helping you?" Sam slapped me. Light flashed as my head smacked against the ground.

Sam's knees pinned my arms. I wiggled, trying to buck him off.

Sam slapped me again, blood warming my cheek. "Why isn't he helping me with girls?" Sam was at the same all-boys high school I was, kept far from any eligible members of the opposite sex.

"Have you asked him?" I said, gently as I could to avoid another slap.

Sam's knees eased off of my arms. "No. He hates me."

"Uncle Pauly doesn't hate you. He got mad at you." I rolled away before I got up, putting a little distance between us. I brushed the grass off the ass of my shorts but my white t-shirt was beyond salvage.

"Why does everyone like you so much?"

It was good that I'd stepped back. I think he would've hit me again if I hadn't.

His question was ridiculous. Three different teachers at our school had come up to me to tell me how impressive Sam was. My Algebra teacher had talked about how smart Sam was in front of my entire class when he realized we were brothers. An English teacher stopped me in the hall to tell me that the highlight of his Friday nights was reading Sam's papers. I wasn't even in his class. When I was in detention for not doing her homework, the Geometry teacher told me that Sam was the best student she'd ever had. I'd caught *Twins* on WB—the one where Arnold Schwarznegger and Danny Devito are genetically engineered so Arnold gets all of the good genes and Danny is the dumping ground for what's left—and immediately recognized Sam and I.

"I messed up things with Ancy, anyway. So we're back on the same square."

I expected him to ask what happened, but instead he turned and headed home. His shoulders collapsed, like I was the one who had jumped him. I can see now that he was badly in need of help, a therapist, an antidepressant, a bear hug. But right then, I hated him so much.

I didn't bother telling Joel about what happened with Ancy or with Sam.

"What happened to your shirt?" he asked.

Mud stains made it a Pollock painting and the neck was stretched beyond repair. I sighed. "Don't worry about it."

We had more pressing issues: his grandpa was watching porn on the computer, so we had to wait. "If you want, I can crack the door and we can watch over his shoulder," he said.

"I'm not watching your grandpa masturbate. It's like Lemon Party." That was a shock site Joel had sent me in an AIM message where three old dudes fucked each other. He'd promised me the boobs from the *Girls Gone Wild* commercials uncensored. I couldn't have clicked that link faster. I nearly threw up.

"I only have one grandpa. We could be like the other two dudes, though."

"You're so gross."

"I took a video at work last night." He showed me on the grainy screen on his flip camera phone. His friend threw some rotten produce in the air, and Joel cut it in half with a machete.

"Don't you get into trouble for doing shit like that?"

"It's rotten anyway. That means it goes to the pig farm,

and the pigs don't care. You want to go out in the yard and throw my ax at the tree?"

Joel worked for two reasons: to help his mom and grandparents with the mortgage, and to buy novelty weapons—knives with blades longer than the legally permitted five inches, butterfly knives, switchblades, knives with jagged edges painted black to look like a Batman insignia, tasers—from a shop in the back corner of the mall's basement. The weapons were illegal under Connecticut state law, but paperweights were permissible, which was how each box advertised the item inside. His latest acquisition was this stupid ax.

It was a dumb fucking idea on a windy day with his wrist still in a cast. I had to give it to him, he hit the tree pretty consistently when the wind didn't carry the ax back toward us. I waited for it to calm on my turn and aimed for the center of the trunk, but the ax clattered to the ground around the roots.

"Did you know, point of fact, that we're aiming for the tree?" he asked.

"I'm trying," I said, but my next two throws hit along the roots too.

Joel was pulling the ax out of the tree when his grandpa, with a little bit of extra pep in his step, yelled out the window, "It's your turn if you still want this thing."

"Great," I said, happy to have made it through another day without having to pull one of Joel's toys out of his thigh.

"Holy shit," Joel said, as the pictures popped up on the screen. "I thought you were fucking with me."

The page with the naked woman getting her heart ripped out was first, followed by six pages of text I'd photographed at random. "How are we going to google them?"

SAY UNCLE

"Dude, I found a forum."

I regret taking those pictures. I regret letting him upload them even more.

CHAPTER 13

Away Message
EnterSamMan88: Told you so.

WE WAITED. SILENTLY, as though someone would respond right away. Joel clicked the refresh button. His grandmother's pink phone, stationed next to the computer, erupted with noise. I jumped.

"Holy shit," Joel said.

The phone rang again.

"How cursed is that book?" Joel asked.

"Answer the phone," Joel's mom yelled through the wall.

Joel rested his hand on the receiver. He looked to me, as if for permission. I nodded and he picked up. Without saying a word, he handed me the phone.

I pressed it to my ear. "Hello?"

"We're on our way," Dad said.

Apparently, he and Mom were picking me up on the way to get Aunt Linda from the train station next to the Subway where Ancy and I had eaten. "Why didn't anyone tell me she was coming?" I asked.

There was a pause. "Didn't you hear us talking about it at dinner last night?" Mom said. They had me on speakerphone while Dad drove. They got a cell, but none for the kids.

They pulled into the driveway and honked.

"We'll talk in the car," Dad said.

"You've gotta go already?" Joel said. He clicked refresh on the computer.

SAY UNCLE

I hung up the phone. "My aunt Linda is here and I need to see her."

"Tell them no," Joel said, as if I could.

"Sorry, dude. Call me later, if anyone says anything about that post." We dapped.

They were in my mom's purple minivan. I rolled the door open and swung into one of the captain's chairs.

"Thanks for the heads up. How come Sam doesn't have to come?"

"We're not talking about your brother. What happened to your shirt?" Mom asked.

The ruined collar hung limp. "We were playing football."

"How many times do I have to tell you?" Mom said, glaring from the front seat. Ever since Matt Alonso broke his ankle, playing football in the vacant lot was banned, but ratting out Sam would only make things worse.

Dad backed out of the driveway.

Joel lived ten minutes from the train station. There were two routes: the four-lane Post Road with a light every hundred yards, and the winding back roads my parents always took. The sidewalk shrunk then disappeared as the road narrowed before it spit us out in front of the Blockbuster.

"How did your date go?" Mom asked.

"Terrible," I said.

My parents exchanged a look, as though I couldn't see them. It reminded me of the way they were still trying to spell out words back when I was ten, as if I wouldn't understand. Or how they thought none of us could crack that "O.T." was code for "over tired."

"I'm sorry to hear that, honey. What happened?"

"I don't want to talk about it."

"You know your uncle isn't the only person who dated around," my dad said.

"Gross. Nobody wants to think of you two out in the world, dating."

We stopped at a red light. I could see the Subway now, and the hardware store. I squinted at the register, trying to get a glimpse of Ancy. I couldn't stop thinking of how badly I'd fucked up, like pressing my tongue against canker sores. Mom turned in her seat, so we could make eye contact.

"Bray, dating is fun, but it's hard, too. The important thing is that with each friend, you're figuring out more of what you want. Maybe this is the end, maybe it's not, but you've got to learn from it. How would you want your future wife to act?"

"You ended up with Dad, so you couldn't have done much figuring," I said.

"Very funny," Dad said. He rolled the car up the platform.

Paul Jr. and Maria flanked Aunt Linda. Her eyes had bags under them, but they lit up as she waved at us.

"She's been alone with those kids," Mom said.

"God bless her," Dad said.

"Braden, you're good with kids. You're going to need to get them away from Uncle Pauly when we get home so he and Aunt Linda can talk," Mom said.

A door slid open. Without a greeting, Aunt Linda asked, "What happened to his shirt?"

"He keeps sneaking off to play football," Mom said.

"After that other boy broke his ankle?" Aunt Linda turned to me. "You saw someone break their ankle and you keep doing what they did?"

"Is anyone hungry? I've got granola bars, apples, and bottles of water," Mom said.

"You live five minutes from here. We can eat at the house," Aunt Linda said, then looked at me and rolled her eyes.

Paul Jr. grabbed my arm. At least he was excited to see me. He'd gotten a compendium of X-Men comics, and he was showing me his favorite panels. Maria, who was five years younger than me, texted God knows who from the backseat when I still didn't have a phone. Aunt Linda and my parents talked about that safe stalwart: the weather.

SAY UNCLE

Conversation trailed off as we got closer to the house. Aunt Linda balled the sides of her blue dress in her fists. Pauly Jr. put his *X-Men* down in the backseat, open to a page of Wolverine facing off against Sabretooth. Maria still had her phone open, but the clicking buttons had slowed to a near stop.

Dad pulled the van into the driveway and broke the silence, "Home sweet home. Welcome everyone."

"Thanks," Aunt Linda said.

Uncle Pauly came outside, scanning the car like some unseen monster was hiding from him. The kids—if not oblivious, then undeterred—ran over my legs to hug their father.

I tried to think of the longest that my dad had been away. He'd gone to Detroit, Columbus, and Buffalo when he was working in sales. He'd go for three or four days at a time, but that was nothing compared to how time must have accordioned out for Maria and Paul Jr. They had no definite end. For them, it might never finish. The world was buzzing with the fact that fifty percent of marriages ended in divorce. It was an inescapable statistic, manifesting in the cultural consciousness—in the newspaper, in the *Late Show* monologues, on the sidelines of soccer games.

"Hey, kids," Uncle Pauly said. He lifted them both up, one in either arm, despite his knees. Maria kissed him on the cheek. Paul Jr. burrowed into his father's neck.

"The kids sure do love him," Aunt Linda said, wistfully, not addressing anyone in particular.

"What a great dad," my mom said louder, projecting for the cheap seats, subtle as a sledgehammer.

Uncle Pauly put the kids down. "Go inside. I'm going to say hi to your mother."

I stayed in the captain's chair, waiting to see the tenor of their reunion, but Dad poked me in the ribs. "Go. Go with the kids. This is private. And you're on the clock tonight, anyway."

71

"It's in our driveway and I'm not getting paid."

"If you want to get a cent of allowance money, you better hope I forget you said that."

Maria and Paul Jr. had run up to Leslie's room and crouched under her open window. Leslie put a finger over her lips as she waved me over. I knelt behind them. Downstairs, my parents came inside, ceding the driveway to Uncle Pauly and Aunt Linda. We couldn't see out the window, but we could hear everything.

The kids were probably expecting a *Parent Trap* situation, but instead overheard Aunt Linda talking about the police. "They were back. They're not so sure it was a suicide anymore."

"I didn't have anything to do with it. You think, what? That I was whispering to her through the pipes?" Uncle Pauly asked.

"You don't need to convince me. I don't know how you talked me into renting that place. I don't want to live anywhere someone did . . . what she did. Or what somebody did to her."

"Who do I need to convince then? If I'm a suspect, then I'm a suspect. I didn't do anything."

"Didn't do anything that anyone could prove."

Paul Jr.'s face crinkled, like he was going to cry. Maria covered his mouth.

"For the last time, I didn't have anything to do with it. She got depressed. She was a lesbian from Iowa. Mommy and Daddy didn't love her enough and then..."

"Do you hear yourself when you talk?"

"Keep it down."

Paul Jr. was crying now, but Maria kept him quiet. Leslie held Maria's hand, covering her own mouth.

"You don't want them to know that you're a suspect. Police are asking for you, and I'm telling them you're with your sister in Connecticut. I'm not lying for you. Not again."

"Why are you telling them where I am? You want me to go to prison? Or get killed in custody?"

"Go see your kids."

"Do they know about any of this?"

"No. They're in the dark. And I'm not letting them . . . up there. We've been hearing noises, like somebody pacing around."

Paul Jr. pulled away from Maria and sobbed. Someone was coming up the stairs.

"Leslie, grab Life," I said.

She slid the box out from under her bed. I moved it to the center of the room and dumped the different pieces on the floor.

Dad knocked a beat on the door, the lame one he tapped to try to be cool.

I motioned for Paul Jr. to stop crying. Maria and Leslie were flipping the pieces as fast as they could, affixing the spinner with its plastic mountains to the board.

"Come in," I said.

Dad surveyed the scene. "Everything okay in here?" He zeroed in on Paul Jr as the rest of us nodded emphatically.

"Paul? Did Braden do something?"

Great. I was going to take the blame for this too.

"Braden didn't do anything. It was me," Maria said.

Dad raised his eyebrows. "What happened?"

"He wanted to play Monopoly," Leslie said.

"I didn't want to play a girl game," Paul Jr. said. He sniffled.

"Sometimes that's the way it is, buddy. Your dad is cooking lamb chops for dinner, and then he's going to take you both for a surprise." Dad paused on his way out. "Braden, why do I have to tell you to change your ruined shirt?"

After I returned in a clean shirt, we idly spun the wheel and tapped the plastic cars along the well-trod paths as

Maria and Paul Jr. filled us in on more details. When the police had found their upstairs neighbor, one of them had vomited in the hallway. Instead of cleaning it up, the head officer designated it the spot for the rest of the department to throw up if they needed to. That way they wouldn't "contaminate the scene."

"And Ms. Harriet has been visiting Maria," Paul Jr. said, more excited than he should've been.

"What?" Leslie said. She was fascinated with ghosts, and convinced that we had one living in the attic. One night she had a sleepover, and she and her friends broke the attic door opening it with a broom. All they found up there was insulation. Paint dripped all over the hardwood floor below when they tried to conceal the damage to the door.

"It's true," Maria said, decidedly less excited than the rest of us.

"How does she manifest?" Leslie asked.

"When Maria looks in the mirror, she sees Ms. Harriet instead," Paul Jr. said.

Maria spun, then moved her car four spaces. She ignored the instructions on the board. "She says she wants me to come upstairs. She wants me to be with her. She'll comb my hair again, like she used to when I was a little girl and she helped babysit us."

"You're not going to go up there, are you?" I said.

"No. Since Dad left, Mom has been locking it. She says that it's a bad place now."

"Good," I said, withholding my own bit of the story. They didn't need to know about their dad's book or the diagrams in it. "Did the upstairs neighbor, did she say anything about what happened to her? Or if your dad . . . "

"We should go there and have a seance," Leslie said, voice high with excitement.

Had she not heard the same conversation?

"That is the best idea. Maybe Mom will take you back into the city with us for the rest of the summer," Maria said.

SAY UNCLE

"Did Ms. Harriet say anything about Uncle Pauly 'whispering through the pipes'?"

"As if," Leslie said, and rolled her eyes.

Paul Jr. shook his head. "I'm going to see if Dad needs help cooking."

"That's a great idea," Maria said, glaring at me.

Before I could say anything, the two of them were on their way downstairs.

I followed them, trying to run interference. The phone rang as I headed downstairs where Aunt Linda and my mom were at the table with glasses of wine. Uncle Pauly stood over the oven, lamb steaming up the room, making my mouth water.

"Braden," Dad said.

I waited for the ensuing fit. I'd lost containment of the kids.

Instead, he held the phone out to me. "It's Joel," he said, pronouncing his name like the piano man even though he'd known Joel for years. "Be quick."

"Dad!" Paul Jr. yelled.

"Paul Jr!" Uncle Pauly yelled, and they were hugging again. Maria got in there, too, as I took the portable phone upstairs.

"Dude, I can't talk. Family's here."

"Don't care." He sounded out of breath. "That post, I've gotten like a hundred emails."

"Already? It's been like an hour."

"I know. They want to see more of the book." He sighed. "Some of them got my cell phone number."

"*How*?"

"Just listen. One of them said he was coming to get the book. He emailed me *my* street address. He says he's in New Jersey. Two hours away."

"Fuck." Everyone in the room stopped what they were doing to look at me. I mumbled an apology.

Dad was gearing up for a lecture on language when Uncle Pauly interrupted to announce dinner was ready.

CHAPTER 14

Away Message
bigRican787: Anybody wants to come to my house, I've got like a hundred knives and a motherfucking throwing ax. I'll cut you.

I SHAMBLED THROUGH the aroma to the table, imagining a pedophile with black leather gloves going after Joel with a silenced pistol. My mouth wasn't watering any longer. For all of his "paperweight" knives and bluster, his lighters and hairspray bottles, Joel didn't have anything that could stop a bullet.

"Was that Ancy?" Sam said, singing her name.

"No. It was Joel," I said, too zombified to take his bait.

"Who's Ancy?" Aunt Linda asked.

"Nobody," I said. I slunk into my regular spot next to Leslie with Paul Jr. and Maria squeezed between us on folding chairs. The worst part of being small was the expectation that you'd shrink to accommodate everyone else.

"Braden's got a girlfriend," Leslie said.

Our cousins caught on quick, singing it as a chorus.

"And what's she like?" Aunt Linda asked.

"She's mad at me," I said, wishing that I could be anywhere else, talking about anything but Ancy.

"Oooh, Braden's in trouble," Sam said, as if we hadn't talked about this hours earlier.

"I asked her to speak her language, so I could hear it," I said, keeping my eyes on the food in front of me—fried

76

lamb chop, asparagus spears, and lovingly buttered hasselback potatoes.

"So?" Sam asked.

"Did you try apologizing?" Aunt Linda asked.

"No," Uncle Pauly said. His knife and fork froze over his food. "Braden's not going to apologize."

"Oh, forgive me. I forgot that men don't apologize," Aunt Linda said.

"What Braden's got to do is make her wait. When you fight in a relationship, that's what you do. It's not about who was right or wrong. It's about who can hold out the longest."

Aunt Linda rolled her eyes. "Hold out what? What the hell happened to you?"

Uncle Pauly continued, "I've seen the way she looks at Bray. She likes him, and she's going to come back to him as long as he keeps ignoring her."

"Is that what you think is going to happen?" Aunt Linda asked, voice tight with spite. "You think this Ancy girl is so pathetic she's going to come running back after Braden's been gone for a week?"

"Who are you going to listen to, Braden? You going to apologize or you going to make her wait?"

Suddenly everyone's attention was on me again. I poked at the potatoes with my fork, hoping for a distraction. Sam was running his hands through his hair. Leslie was chewing her nails.

"It was a hot one today," Dad said.

"The high was ninety-four," Mom added.

"It's what she should do. Is she going to work in that hardware store for the rest of her life? She needs someone to take care of her," Uncle Pauly said.

Maria's lower lip quivered. Paul Jr. was watching her, not sure how to react.

Uncle Pauly's knife clicked against his plate. He cut that lamb like it owed him money. The noise broke the dam of Maria's tears. Paul Jr. followed suit, but no one else seemed to notice.

"Is that what you think, you motherfucker?" Aunt Linda asked. She set her glass down with a loud clunk, water sloshing over the rim.

Dad cleared his throat. "I prefer the cold. You can always put more layers on, but you can't take off that much."

Everyone else's heads were down.

Uncle Pauly's face was red. He looked at Aunt Linda with narrowed eyes. "It's what I know."

"I'll tell you what I know, you piece of shit." Aunt Linda balled up the napkin she was using to clean up the spilled water in one fist, as if entertaining the idea of throwing it at him.

"Not in front of the kids." Mom put a hand on Aunt Linda's shoulder.

"I know that you haven't worked in four years. I tell you to see a therapist—"

"Not this again," Uncle Pauly said.

"No. You don't get to fucking say that." Aunt Linda stood up. "This family and all its secrets. It would've been okay for you to take some time to deal with your . . . whatever, but you never did. It's been four years."

"Therapy," he sneered, crossing his arms.

"I don't care if it's therapy, or church, or a life coach, a support group, or whatever else you can find, but you need to do something for me. For Maria and Paul." She waved an arm toward their crying children. "Instead you walk around, picking fights. Wasting my money on God knows what. Whatever you've been through doesn't excuse what you've done. There are plenty of people who lost family and friends and aren't walking around like an open wound."

"Shut up," Uncle Pauly said, his voice savage, low with anger.

Dad waved his hands like a referee. "I think this has gone far enough."

In my mind, I saw it escalating further. I imagined Uncle Pauly palming Dad's face and shoving him to the ground before going after Aunt Linda.

SAY UNCLE

Uncle Pauly did stand. "Kids, I love you, but it's time for you to go back to the city." His fork, planted in a piece of lamb, tipped over.

"But we just got here," Paul Jr. said, voice tiny.

"Hey," Uncle Pauly said, sharply, "You're a man. No crying."

"What about the surprise?" Maria asked.

But Uncle Pauly was up the stairs, yelling, "Get them on the next train," as if this were his house, not my parents'.

Aunt Linda cradled her face in her hands.

Paul Jr. slapped himself to stop his tears. When it didn't work, he slapped himself again.

"Don't let him do that, Braden," Mom said.

I grabbed Paul Jr.'s wrist. At first he struggled, but then he burrowed his head into my chest, dampening my clean shirt with his tears and snot.

"Well that was awkward," Sam said.

"Are you okay?" Dad asked Aunt Linda. "We're not rushing you out. You can stay as long as you like."

"We're not taking sides," Mom said.

Aunt Linda held a hand up to stop them from saying any more. "We'll finish our dinner and then we'll go."

"There's really no reason—"

Aunt Linda jerked her head toward my dad. "Goddamnit. I said we're finishing our dinners and then leaving."

Sam and I stayed home while my parents and Leslie dropped our New York family at the train station. There was so much happening, I couldn't focus. Ancy hated me. Someone was on their way to hurt Joel. Uncle Pauly and Aunt Linda had always seemed like the happiest couple out of my mom's siblings. Even at Christmas that year, they'd seemed to be the most in love, and now they were breaking up.

I would love to tell you that I rushed over to protect my best friend. That's what I should've done. But all of the stress overloaded me, like a blender stuffed so full the blade can't turn. It still happens to me sometimes. When the world overwhelms me, I turn off. My therapist calls it Dorsal Vagal Shutdown.

Whatever you want to call it, Sam and I gravitated to the TV. I let it absorb me as Sam flipped between the Yankees game and *Simpsons* reruns. With everything on my mind, I just needed to shut off.

When both were on a commercial, Sam turned the volume down and looked at me. "Do you want to hear the 9/11 story?"

Of course I did.

"Uncle Pauly's restaurant opened at 11, but Pauly got there at 9 every morning.

"The first plane hit fifteen minutes before he got there. The subways were all shutting down, so he went to the restaurant and turned on the TV. Every channel was showing the footage of the plane hitting the first tower again and again. Uncle Pauly is so caught up, he doesn't think to call the 'morning girl.' She's scheduled to come in at 10.

"She wasn't even coming in to do anything important. She was going to fold napkins and chop onions and tomatoes with Uncle Pauly. He didn't really need her, and I think that's the part that really tears Uncle Pauly up.

"But the morning girl was walking from her apartment to the restaurant. There were so many things that could've gone different. Like, if the morning girl had turned on her TV or her radio, she wouldn't have come in. If she had to take the subway or a bus or a cab, she would've been stuck at home.

"I guess the morning girl didn't notice anything was going wrong until the building collapsed."

"Shit," I said quietly. I remembered waiting in line at

my middle school to use the office phone to check if Uncle Pauly was okay. Kids in my class had lost parents.

"Yeah," Sam said.

A hush fell over both of us. Sam turned the noise up on the TV. Randy Johnson notched another strike out. I was imagining what it must've been like for Uncle Pauly. Did he hear the noise of the building imploding or see it on the news first?

Then the doorbell rang.

CHAPTER 15

Away Message
Number1AvrilLavigneFanSoComplicated:
Surprise cousin visit RUINED!!! Why can't adults solve their problems without yelling???

J.OEL WAS AT the door, shrunk with fear.

"That guy from New Jersey is on his way to my house. Like, right now."

"What guy from New Jersey?" Sam asked.

I hadn't wanted to let Sam in on the guy from New Jersey or Uncle Pauly's book. "Don't worry—"

"Your uncle Pauly has got this magic book and we took pictures of it and uploaded the pages to a forum and now this guy from New Jersey is coming to kill my family so he can take the book."

"Magic book?" Sam asked.

"Yes. Keep up," Joel said to Sam. Then to me, "You got me into this."

"Keep it down," I said. I'd grown up in the room Uncle Pauly was in. It wasn't exactly soundproof.

"Dude, I don't want to fight some neckbeard in my front yard. We need to get the book."

"Uncle Pauly already suspects I know."

Sam's voice ramped up as he said, "Joel's family is in trouble because of you and you're not going to help him?"

"It's not that I don't want to help him," I said. My mind raced to complete the phrase. But I don't want to get in trouble? But then Uncle Pauly will know I lied? But what?

"Then what do you want?" Joel said. His eyes said more, that he'd tried to help me.

"Do you think we could do something without telling Uncle Pauly?"

Sam grabbed my arm and shoved me toward the stairs. I stopped arguing.

The three of us trudged up to Uncle Pauly's room. Joel and Sam shoved me to the front. My "Danger: Braden's Room" sign was barely hanging onto the chipped white paint of the door.

I lifted my hand, then paused. Trying to think of what I could say to solve this another way. Before I could, Sam pounded on the door like a cop serving a warrant.

The floor creaked in the room. No turning back now. I was breathing but my lungs didn't feel like they were taking in any air. The door burst open. Uncle Pauly's eyes were bloodshot. I half expected him to come out swinging. He looked over the three of us, pausing on Joel, who he'd met but probably didn't remember.

"What?"

Joel and Sam were tongue-tied, but Sam worked a knuckle into my kidney, forcing me toward Uncle Pauly.

"We need your help."

Uncle Pauly sighed. "What did you do?"

The question jarred Joel loose, and he rattled off what we'd done with the forum. Uncle Pauly bore a hole through me as Joel talked.

"Now that you're waist-deep in shit, you're honest with me," Uncle Pauly said. He shook his head.

"We just want the book," Joel said.

"Who is this guy from New Jersey? Do you know his name?" Uncle Pauly asked.

"People don't post on forums with their real names," Sam said, oh so helpfully.

"His username was Screecher72," Joel said.

Uncle Pauly nodded. "Okay. I know him." Then he closed the door to my room.

We only had forty-five minutes now. We had to do something. I imagined this man from New Jersey attacking Joel's mother. His grandfather. It would be my fault. I brought this into Joel's life.

"Is he going to help us?" Joel asked.

Neither Sam nor I answered.

"Knock again," Joel said.

"You knock," Sam said.

"Dude," Joel said, and shoved me forward.

"C'mon, Braden," Sam said, jostling me closer to the door.

I reached up to do it, but I was knocking on air as the door swung back open. Uncle Pauly stood there, black robe wrapped around him like he was a B-movie vampire. He clutched the book to his chest.

"Let's go."

He moved through us like a shadow and went down the stairs. Sam and Joel pushed in front of me now, and I had to jog to keep up.

"What are we going to do?" Joel asked.

"Are we going to fuck him up?" Sam asked.

Uncle Pauly grabbed Dad's keys and tossed them to Sam. "You're driving," he said.

Sam nodded. He and Joel were tense, fists balled, faces tight. They marched like they were headed off to war. I was scared. I was sure they were, too, but they seemed to funnel the fear into anger.

We piled into Dad's car. "This dude thinks he can come into our neighborhood," Sam said, as if there was any camaraderie between us and anyone in our community. He backed out onto the street.

"He wants to come in here and go after my family," Joel said. He cracked the knuckles on his uncasted hand.

Sam turned on the radio. AC/DC's "If You Want Blood

SAY UNCLE

(You've Got It)" blared on the classic rock station. He'd spent his summer working at Burger King to pay for the stereo. The subwoofer rattled the glass as Bon Scott screeched over the Young brothers' guitars.

Uncle Pauly turned it off. "Guys. I'm going to give Screecher the book."

"What?" they said together.

"Eyes on the road, Sam," Uncle Pauly said.

"You put on that bathrobe to give a troll your book? Someone threatens my family and you're going to play dress up?"

Uncle Pauly shook his head. "You want me to what, kill him on your front lawn? And then what? Go to prison?"

Relief washed over me. I didn't want to see a fight.

Sam pulled to a complete stop at the stop sign. He turned on his right blinker, and checked three times before turning onto the road between Joel's and ours.

"I just figured . . . " Joel started.

"This is good. The right decision," I said. If Uncle Pauly gave the book away, it wouldn't be in my house anymore. The magic-book-bound-in-human-flesh portion of my summer would be over.

"Why did you want us to come then?" asked Sam. He took the final turn onto Joel's street.

"I didn't. You were all riled up and I didn't want to drive," Uncle Pauly said.

Joel ran his hands through his hair. "So this guy won't kill my family?"

"I don't see why he would once he got the book," Uncle Pauly said.

Sam pulled up to the curb. The four of us got out and leaned against the car. The heat of the day had broken, and a breeze cooled us. Mosquitos buzzed and crickets chirped. Joel took out a joint and lit it. He offered it to Uncle Pauly, who rejected it. I passed too. Sam took two puffs before Uncle Pauly intercepted it.

"Your mom know you smoke?" Uncle Pauly asked, smirking.

"I don't," I said.

"No," Sam said.

"It's true. Braden doesn't," Joel said.

"Look, Braden, Sam, I want you both to go home," Uncle Pauly said. "And Joel"—saying it the American way—"go inside. I'll talk to Screecher on my own."

Uncle Pauly threw Joel's joint on the ground and stomped it out.

"You sure?" Sam asked.

"I don't need back up, especially not from a couple of high schoolers," Uncle Pauly said. "No offense."

Sam rankled. Joel stared at the stomped-out joint. I walked around to the passenger side of the car.

"Go," Uncle Pauly said.

A pair of headlights spread our shadows on the concrete. A Buick turned onto the street. It slowed, heading toward us.

"Be safe," Uncle Pauly said.

I climbed into the passenger seat and slammed my door shut. Sam hesitated, then followed. Joel took another look at his wasted weed, then headed toward the door, shaking his head.

Sam was half-out, half-in when Uncle Pauly knocked on the hood of the car. Sam finally got in. Uncle Pauly closed Sam's door the rest of the way, then walked toward what must've been Screecher's car.

Screecher flashed his high beams twice. Uncle Pauly held up a hand, signaling for him to wait. Then he waved Sam and I through like a traffic cop.

"This isn't right," Sam said.

"Let him protect us," I said.

Sam didn't say anything else as we drove down the street. He slowed next to the Buick. Screecher was a white dude in his thirties or forties wearing a red and blue baseball cap with a logo I didn't recognize. His hair was long and tangled, sweeping his shoulders. He hadn't shaved in a while. Sam glared, while Screecher assessed, then dismissed us.

Sam sped up. When we passed the curve, he turned the lights off and parked the car.

"What are you doing?" I asked.

"We're not leaving Pauly alone with that guy."

CHAPTER 16

Away Message
BrayDay327: Just when you think things
can't get worse. Fuck everything!

T HERE WAS A path through the woods between
Joel's backyard and the street where Sam parked. At
Halloween, Joel's family put up plastic skeletons and
we doused ourselves in fake blood to jump out at the
neighborhood kids. I didn't need the lights to get us back
to Joel's.

I led Sam slowly along the path, pointing at the places
where roots stuck up or the ground divotted. I didn't want
to go, but I couldn't abandon Sam. It was so dumb.
Screecher could have a gun. And then what could we do?
Get shot to death with Uncle Pauly? It wasn't like the
alternative was better, though.

I also had this nagging fear: what if the book worked?
Could it be worse than a gun?

I moved at half-speed, hoping that Uncle Pauly would
give the damn thing away by the time we got there. We'd
watch Screecher drive away and then race to beat Uncle
Pauly home.

We saw Uncle Pauly first, clutching the book to his chest.

Screecher came into view, an unkempt man with a
perpetual mean look in his eyes. There wasn't any obvious
sign that he was armed. I couldn't hear what he was saying
yet, but I could hear the squeak in his voice that must've
been where his nickname came from.

SAY UNCLE

As we got closer, their voices became clearer. "You can buy a book with your wife's trust fund, but you can't buy power."

"I know," Uncle Pauly said.

"Then you let some kids find it and upload the pictures. You're an idiot. Give it to me." Screecher flapped his arms.

"Can I ask you something first?"

"I've got a long drive," Screecher said. He stretched his back, bending down.

Sam and I crouched at the end of the trees, ready to run at them. Sam tapped my shoulder and pointed to the right. Joel hadn't gone inside, either. He was sneaking along the side of the house, back pressed against the wall. His throwing ax dangled from his good hand.

"What are you going to do with the book?" Uncle Pauly asked.

"What am I going to do with the book? Whatever the hell I want. What were you doing with it?"

"Buy and sell weasels like you."

"You could have paid for the kid's funeral. Too late now, though."

Joel stopped edging along the house. He lifted the ax.

"I don't much like the idea of my nephew losing his best friend." He glanced over at Joel.

The air in front of Screecher's hands shimmered, like gas was shooting in front of it. Green orbs of light ignited, radiating out of Screecher's hands.

What the hell was that?

"You don't have much of a choice," Screecher said.

"You've got all the natural ability in the world. But you're an idealist."

"What's that supposed to mean?" Screecher asked.

"You're posturing. You've got this cool looking green stuff, but you've never used it. You've never killed anyone. It's all theoretical, and you're trying to tell me that you're going to kill me if I don't give you this book, and then

89

you're going to explode that family. Meanwhile, you've never even punched someone in the face."

"What's that got to do with anything?"

Uncle Pauly was a foot taller than Screecher and probably fifty pounds heavier. He took two steps forward and hit Screecher with a right. Screecher crashed onto the hood of his car. Uncle Pauly wound up to hit him again. Maybe he didn't need our help.

"Idiot," Screecher said, blood trickling from his busted lip. The green light knitted itself into tendrils, thick as a fire hose. They snapped around Uncle Pauly's wrists and ankles, lifting him into the air.

Uncle Pauly writhed to break free.

Screecher pushed himself off the hood of the Buick as the green ropes forced Uncle Pauly to kneel on the pavement. Uncle Pauly groaned.

"Now," Uncle Pauly said, looking at Joel again.

"What?" Screecher asked, confidence flickering. Finally turning in Joel's direction.

But it was too late. Joel's ax was tumbling through the air toward Screecher. The throw was longer than the ones we normally made for the tree, but with Joel's family on the line, he caught Screecher in the jaw with the blunt side of the ax. Screecher's green light disappeared as he grabbed his chin. We charged.

Screecher generated more of his magic light. He aimed at Joel and Sam and me.

It snapped toward us, but before it hit, Uncle Pauly was on top of Screecher. He said something in a language I didn't understand. Uncle Pauly shoved his free arm into Screecher's mouth. Yes, *into*. First Uncle Pauly's hand went in, then the elbow, until he was shoulder-deep in Screecher. It was impossible. From the outside, you couldn't see a thing, but Uncle Pauly's arm had to be going somewhere.

Screecher's eyes went so wide they looked about to burst. The rest of that green aura dispersed. The moss smell from Uncle Pauly's apartment invaded the air around us.

SAY UNCLE

"If you were going to stay alive, I'd want you to remember that you thought I was a talentless, dumb jock."

Screecher mumbled something, words garbled by the obstruction.

Then Uncle Pauly yanked his arm out. There was a terrible ripping noise, like a sheet being torn in two, as Screecher turned inside out. A wet mess of guts slopped onto the street. Even from ten yards away, Screecher's inside were the worst thing I'd ever smelled. Fear bolted me in place.

"What the fuck," Joel yelled, pointing at Uncle Pauly.

"Where are the bones?" Sam asked, then threw up.

Uncle Pauly's robe turned a darker shade of black from the blood. With his clean arm, the one that hadn't been inside Screecher, he pulled the robe over his head and used it to cover what was left of Screecher.

There wasn't a force on this earth or the next that could've protected his boots, but the cloak had kept his clothing relatively clean.

"Stay there," he said. "And actually listen this time."

He took out the skull dagger Paul Jr. showed me in the upstairs of their apartment. "He couldn't have died on the grass?" he muttered, before carving a circle around what was left of Screecher. He said something else in that guttural language. The moss smell returned, strong enough to overpower the stink of Screecher's insides. A yellow dot appeared in the center. It spread evenly to the edges. I caught a glimpse through that hole and saw a marble slab with chains on it. The viscera and the cloak fell through. Blood splattered on the altar.

Uncle Pauly said something else, and the disk disappeared, taking the mossy smell with it.

"Holy shit," Joel said. "Your uncle's a motherfucking sorcerer."

Sam fell to his knees, clutching his stomach.

Then Uncle Pauly collapsed.

91

CHAPTER 17

Away Message
bigRican787: Getting Wendy's at Pilot with the other stoners 420

SAM WENT THROUGH the woods to get the car. He threw up again when he thought he'd gotten out of earshot. I sat on the curb next to Uncle Pauly, who was laying on the asphalt. Joel traced the spot the yellow disk had been with his fingers.

"It's cold," he whispered.

If you'd asked me what I thought I'd feel if I saw someone being murdered, I would have imagined screaming. But instead, I felt a deep numbness. I had a sense that it was like nitroglycerin inside me. Jostle me in any direction and I'd detonate. Maybe tears. Maybe anger. I didn't really want to find out.

Joel kept investigating the spot on the ground, hyperfixating. "Didn't even leave a mark."

Headlights illuminated all three of us as Sam brought the car around the block.

It took both me and Joel to get Uncle Pauly back on his feet. Uncle Pauly was a dead weight, a two-hundred-and-fifty-pound sack of meat. He muttered a stream of nonsense, too quiet to understand.

Sam stopped in front of us and flung the passenger door open. When we'd finally maneuvered Uncle Pauly's ass into the seat, I felt buoyant, almost like I would float away. Then I remembered what Uncle Pauly had done to

Screecher. That I'd seen a man's organs slap onto the road.

"Braden," Sam said, and snapped in my face.

Uncle Pauly had slumped forward. As we went to sit him up, he got louder, clearer, for a second. "We need to do something about the car."

Joel and I wrestled him back up and buckled him in.

In front of us, Screecher's car idled. The yellowish tint of his New Jersey plates glowed under Sam's headlights.

Uncle Pauly's head bobbed back down.

In movies it always seems simple, to take a car down to the dock and drive it into the ocean. Neither Joel nor I had driven before. Sam couldn't drive two cars at once.

My brother looked like he might hurl again any second as he rolled down the passenger side window and asked, "Where do we put the car?"

"The mall parking lot? Drive it over, find a dark corner, and no one is going to notice at least until morning." Joel said.

"The security will find it overnight," I said. I'd seen them circling the empty parking lot on the way home from a midnight movie earlier that summer.

"What's open twenty-four hours?" Joel tapped his casted wrist on the roof of the car, then yanked it back and rubbed it.

"The Pilot," I said.

Pilot was a truck stop with a combination Wendy's and convenience store. The intercom chimed, "Shower stall number 17 is now available," every five or ten minutes. We were too young to go to bars or sex shops after everything else closed at eleven, so we'd hang out there if we could bum a ride. No one would notice a couple of teenagers pulling up in two cars and leaving in one.

"They've got cameras," Sam said.

"Yeah, but there's a corner where they can't see," Joel said.

"How do you know that?" I asked.

"My dealer works the register at Wendy's, so he sells there."

"Do we take Uncle Pauly home first?" I asked.

"Not while Mom and Dad are awake," Sam said, leaning over Uncle Pauly in the passenger seat to talk out the window.

"But who's going to drive Screecher's car?" I asked.

Joel walked toward the car. "Tonight sucked, but at least I'm going to get to drive."

"Stop! You're going to get your fingerprints all over the car," I said.

"Braden's right," Sam said.

Joel paused at the driver's side door. "You guys know that the police need to have my fingerprints in their system for that to matter, right? They can't take every Puerto Rican kid's fingerprints just in case, even if they want to."

Sam and I both shut up for a minute. *CSI* had done a number on us.

"Wouldn't you want to wear gloves, just in case?" Sam asked. "Like, if they ask you later on."

"Nah," Joel said, and plopped into the car.

I went in the car with Sam and Uncle Pauly. Joel followed us.

I sat in the back seat. The moment replayed in my head, over and over.

"What did we see?" Sam asked.

"I don't know," I said.

I looked to Uncle Pauly for answers as he mumbled in the passenger seat.

"Was it real?" Sam asked.

I didn't answer him. I really didn't know.

SAY UNCLE

We were going to leave Uncle Pauly in the car, but he revived enough to tell us he'd be safer inside with us. So Sam and I helped Uncle Pauly, mumbling still, but fitting in perfectly with the night-time crowd at the Pilot, sleep-deprived truckers calling it quits and stoners satisfying their munchies. We slid him into a booth, dried-but-still-bloodstained boots and all. Joel had parked on the other side of the station and came through the convenience store section of the building into the Wendy's.

He didn't see the cop, the only cop in the city that I knew, behind him.

Officer Shelley was in charge of doing the anti-drug presentations in the public schools, though she'd peppered my class with stories of her divorce as well. She had filled our elementary-school heads with stories of kids dying from asthma attacks after their first puff of marijuana, the slippery slope it would take us down to crack and heroin. She screened surrealist movies where kids who died in drunk-driving accidents looked out into the world of the living and complained about the horrible nature of death. Of course, none of it had any impact on Joel, or the majority of other kids in our town.

"I love driving," he said.

I tried to signal him with my eyes, to make a face that would get him to shut the fuck up, but of course he didn't pick up on it.

"I can't wait to get my license."

Officer Shelley, a red head in her street blues, tapped his shoulder.

Joel's smile faded.

"I see you're doing well, Mr. Mancinas," Officer Shelley said. Her recall impressed the shit out of me.

Joel turned slowly.

She looked at me and Sam next. "Mr. O'Riley and Mr. O'Riley," she said, a terse greeting. "If I remember correctly, you've got another year before you can drive legally, Mr. Mancinas."

"I didn't drive. We came from the arcade," Joel said.

Officer Shelley crossed her arms.

"Funzi's Arcade," I added. "Sam drove, and he's got his license."

"Exactly," Sam said, and took out his wallet to show her.

"Which arcade, again?" she asked.

"Funzi's," Joel said, looking back at us. We nodded vigorously.

"Interesting." She folded her arms. "So you'd be aware that Funzi's was closed tonight for a private event, and since you were there, you'd be able to tell me the nature of the event."

"Of course," Joel said. "It was a birthday party."

Officer Shelley upped the ante. "For who?"

The birthday was an easy guess. I kept my mouth shut, hoping Joel could come up with something.

Joel leaned in conspiratorially. "I know we're not supposed to, but we crashed the party. I said hi to a couple of people like we knew them, grabbed some tokens, and we played some racing games."

Officer Shelley stared at him, unblinking. "It's not illegal. Why don't any of you look like you had fun?"

"We got kicked out," Joel said, and turned his back on her. He directed Sam and I into the line to buy Wendy's, where the cashier was disinterestedly watching our conversation with Officer Shelley.

"And who's that with you?" Officer Shelley asked.

Before we could turn around, she was headed for Uncle Pauly, who was slouched on the table, mumbling incoherently. His boots were obscured under the table. I pictured her seeing them, arresting us.

"That's their uncle," Joel said.

"Was he at that party with you, too?" Officer Shelley asked. She tapped her fingers three times on the table in front of Uncle Pauly. "Excuse me, sir?" She tapped three more times.

SAY UNCLE

Uncle Pauly lifted his head up. "It all has a cost," he said, the clearest his murmurings had gotten since he told us to bring him inside. He leaned back, stretching his legs forward.

"Sir, have you been drinking this evening?" Officer Shelley asked, not commenting on his bloodstained boots, popping out the other side of the bench. I slid in to block her view.

"I was driving," Sam said.

The stoners who hung out at the Pilot were watching, some edging for the door while the braver stayed to get a laugh. The truckers, easily identifiable by being over twenty-five and not reeking of pot, were less interested, but one in the corner watched like this was a sitcom.

"So?" Officer Shelley asked, this time turning toward Sam with her hands on her hips, her right above her gun. She wasn't reaching for it, but its presence was loud with possibilities.

I shoved Uncle Pauly's feet off the bench, then slid over the spot they'd left.

"That means he wasn't doing anything illegal," Sam said.

"He's drunk as hell, but there's no law against that," Joel added.

"I know you were in my class, and thus were at least at one point explained the concept of drunk and disorderly," Officer Shelley said. "Not to mention endangering minors."

"He's not disorderly," I said, trying to keep from yelling.

"There was no scene before you got here," Joel said.

He was good at lying to a certain point, but now he needed to shut the fuck up.

Officer Shelley tapped the table again. "Sir," she said. "I'm going to need you to answer some questions."

"We're going to get him some food while we wait for *time*, the only thing that brings sobriety," Sam said.

Officer Shelley raised her eyebrows. "O'Riley, you remember that?"

"Yeah," said Sam. For once his smarts were good for something.

97

"And yet I still find you here, at the truck stop with an uncle who can barely stand. Help me make some sense of it. You're a smart kid. What are you wasting your time here for if you're not on drugs?"

"It's the only place that's open," I said.

Officer Shelley stopped tapping on the table in front of Uncle Pauly.

"And look, I know my uncle's drunk," I said. "But he's going through a hard time. He and his wife are separated and he's been staying with us. We're going to get him a triple cheeseburger, and we're going to get him home." I hoped this would work.

Sam gave me a dirty look.

"He's getting divorced," Officer Shelley said, soaking the information in. "Sorry to hear that, O'Riley."

Okay. This was something. "Yeah. His kids visited today. It was the first time he's seen them this week," I said.

Officer Shelley's hand came off the table.

"He's really broken up about it," I said.

Sam looked like he was ready to kill me, but Officer Shelley was loosening up. "Get him fed, and get him home. Don't let me catch him like this again."

We ordered enough food for eight people and sat with it in absolute silence. Uncle Pauly managed to lift his head up and take a fry or two, but his burger went unbitten. None of us had any appetite. I tried a fry and it tasted like nothing but I chowed down half a burger. When we finished, we drove around town to kill time until after our parents' 10 o'clock bedtime.

All of us made stabs at talking about what Uncle Pauly had done for us, but we kept backing off. Like cars playing chicken. No one wanted to talk about it while the man who did it was riding shotgun, even if he was incoherent.

We dropped Joel off and lugged Uncle Pauly up to bed.

Downstairs, there was a purple sticky note at my place on the table.

Ancy had called.

CHAPTER 18

Away Message
BrayDay327: I need everything to be okay.
When is it going to get better?

IT WAS TOO LATE to call anyone—and, anyway, what would I have said? "My uncle Pauly killed a guy with magic in my best friend's front yard." I couldn't imagine any reality where Ancy would believe me, or a reality where I wouldn't break down crying as I said it.

Sam climbed into his bed.

I didn't bother to refill the air mattress even though it had deflated so much that my joints were poking the hardwood floor beneath it.

"What did we see?" he asked.

"I don't know," I said. And we left the conversation at that. He whimpered quietly, maybe thinking I couldn't hear him.

I closed my eyes and I was out.

In my dream, Paul Jr. led me through the closet in the upstairs apartment, but something was off about him. His gaze was empty. He couldn't hear me. The thing leading me was hollowed out. Paul Jr.'s body with something else behind the wheel.

It didn't talk, but showed me through the closet, into the dark room. The moss smell mixed with decay overwhelmed me.

My hand automatically searched the wall for the light switch. Before I found it, four torches illuminated a circular stone in the center of the room, about the same size as the one Uncle Pauly had carved into the ground. There was one of those cornucopias—my teacher showed us in the racist videos about the origins of Thanksgiving—in the center. Something resembling grapes hung out of its mouth.

I squinted. Not grapes. A red mess of entrails. Screecher's entrails. Every fiber of my being wanted to run, but I couldn't. It was like I was playing a video game with the controller unplugged.

The source of the mossy smell was cloaked in shadows against the wall.

The Paul Jr. thing held the knife with the skull on the handle. "It's seen you. It won't forget."

I had a thousand questions I couldn't ask. The walls of the rooms faded away. The hollow Paul Jr. disappeared. I floated in a blackness, asleep and powerless, but aware. It was like I was outside of time and space, suspended in that abyss.

I woke up sweaty and shivering, more tired than before I'd gone to sleep.

It's seen you.

My eyelids were heavy at our weekly 9 o'clock Mass. Each time they closed, Mom poked me in the ribs. Normally, I hated it, but that day I appreciated anything that distracted me from Screecher.

I scanned the pews for Ancy, though I rarely saw her at Mass. Her family was CAPE Catholics, showing up only for Christmas, Ash Wednesday, Palm Sunday, and Easter. No chance of seeing them on a Sunday in Ordinary Time.

After church, we went to the Dunkin Donuts drive-thru to swear at the people we'd just done the sign of peace with. If Catholic church taught me anything in the fifteen years my parents dragged me there, it's how quickly the peace and love of Mass transformed into road rage in the poorly designed parking lot.

SAY UNCLE

Ancy's hardware store was only a few blocks from the church, but in the opposite direction as Dunkin. In the car I thought about how badly I'd fucked it up, telling her about teaching Augustine to swear. I willed myself to keep thinking about that, to obsess over it rather than Screecher.

I pictured seeing her in the drive-thru, hopping out of the car and running to her. She'd throw open her door, fall into my arms and we'd kiss in our church clothes, right there between the puddles that never seemed to drain. I saw Screecher's organs float up in the puddle and blinked them away.

Even as we drove home, the Screecher-Ancy dance in my head kept tangoing. I looked for her in the passing cars but saw his face. I wondered if Ancy was feeling the same way about me. I guess that was the point, and I felt guilty, but I'd ignored Uncle Pauly before, and then I'd blown it. This time, I'd take his advice. After what he did last night, how could I ignore him?

The miasma came with something that felt like a fever. There was a voice telling me again and again that I had fucked up, and that because I had fucked up now it meant that I would keep fucking up. By listening to Uncle Pauly and ignoring Ancy until the next evening at the earliest, I was throwing away the best thing in my life.

I didn't imagine seeing Ancy at home, but I was hoping that Uncle Pauly would come downstairs to eat doughnuts with us. The sticky note was all that was there, though— purple, with the adhesive wearing away so a corner stretched up into the air.

Mom went to get him, but when she came down her eyes were full of worry. "Hon, he's not doing well. I think we need to take him to a hospital."

"Are you sure?" Dad asked, dunking the edge of his donut into his coffee.

Mom stared at him.

Dad put down his donut. "Okay. You know your brother. Let's go."

"He says he'll only go if he talks to Braden first."

I trudged up the stairs. The doughnut sat like a rock in my stomach. Uncle Pauly was dangerous, no question about it. He'd said in the car, everything he was doing was for this family, and I was part of it. That constituted a promise not to hurt me. But if everything he was doing was for his family, how could he leave his kids and Aunt Linda? But he'd killed for Joel. Again, I fought off the image of Screecher sloshing onto the pavement.

I tapped on Uncle Pauly's door. He looked like shit, like his skin was candle wax that had melted out of shape.

"I'm paying for it now," he said. "For what I did to that shit weasel." He covered a cough with a fist. "I saved your friend. I saved you and your family, but the price of death is death."

"Oh shit," I said, covering my mouth.

"I wrote down some instructions." He pulled out an envelope from under his pillow. "You need to trade someone for me."

"What?" On some level, I must have understood him, but part of my brain didn't want me to make the connection, some kind of emotional gag reflex preventing the poison from going down.

"It's going to kill me, unless you feed it someone else."

I took the envelope and flipped it over in my hands, as if that would reveal more information. I couldn't kill anybody. But still, I heard myself asking, "Who?"

Uncle Pauly pointed to the desk. "Get it."

I thought of Uncle Pauly turning Screecher inside out. I didn't want to touch the book.

"No good deed goes unpunished with you, huh?" Uncle Pauly said. Another chorus of coughs ripped through him.

The book's skin was leathery, but rather than room temperature as it had been when I touched it before, the book was warm now. It felt moist, almost as though it were lathered with gel.

"It's linked to my appendix," he said. "It's a little trick I picked up. If the magic chooses, it goes where it pleases—hearts, lungs. Then there's no time."

I put the book down on the bed in front of him.

"Sam and Joel don't have girlfriends," Uncle Pauly said. He flipped the book open to the page on human sacrifice that I had uploaded to Joel's forum.

Oh damn. Oh shit. Oh fuck.

"You're going to have plenty of girlfriends. I told you this girl was practice," Uncle Pauly said. "You're going to sow your wild oats."

"I can't," I said, voice low.

"Then—" Another volley of coughs cut Uncle Pauly off. "Let me die. I saved your friend, but just throw me away like yesterday's garbage."

"Uncle Pauly."

"Men provide for their families. They pay back favors. It's what we do." He fought back another cough.

"Does it have to be Ancy?" I liked her. I didn't want to hurt anyone, but I especially didn't want to hurt her. My legs trembled. I balanced myself with the desk.

"Would you rather have it be her or Leslie? Maria? Aunt Linda?"

"Why does it have to be anyone we know?"

Uncle Pauly shook his head. "I killed for you. If you're not decent enough to return the favor, just say so."

"That's not what it is."

"Wait 'til Monday," Uncle Pauly said. "Then you convince Ancy to go to the city with you. Take her to a nice lunch at the restaurant below my apartment, and then head up to the second floor. You've got the rest written out." He gestured toward the envelope in my hands. "Put the book back, but bring it with you when you go."

It was the heaviest piece of paper I'd ever held.

CHAPTER 19

Away Message
BrayDay327: I don't know what to do. I wish someone would come down and help me. I need help.

S AM AND I had to carry Uncle Pauly to the car, but after that the two of us and Leslie were left to fend for ourselves. In other words, to watch whatever we wanted on TV until our parents got back. Leslie wanted to watch *Charmed* reruns but Sam preferred professional bull riding. They bickered back and forth before they turned to me, the deciding vote.

"I don't care. *Charmed*." I got up, feeling like I was outside of my body. As Sam flipped the channel toward the rerun, he passed an overhead shot of Pilot.

"Wait, go back," I said.

Leslie groaned. "Change the channel. Who cares about this?"

An unflapped anchor said. "The latest update on this developing story is that a private investigator has located Mr. Schrader's car in the parking lot of the Pilot Truck Stop in Milford, Connecticut. Anyone with any information is being urged to come forward at this time."

The moment I thought that we couldn't be any more fucked, the news transitioned to a familiar woman in a tan pantsuit heading a press conference. Her son, Peter Schrader, had gone missing.

"Is that Screecher's mom?" I asked.

Sam gaped at the screen. "Fuck, fuck, fuck."

"There will be a handsome reward for any relevant information about the disappearance of my son. I repeat, we have no reason to believe Peter's abduction is in any way related to my reelection campaign. If the individuals responsible are listening, I want them to know that Peter is a good boy. He likes collecting rare books and playing Magic: The Gathering. He wouldn't harm a fly, and I hope that you'll extend that same mercy to him."

I tried not to picture his organs, sloshing onto the street. Some mercy.

Sam turned off the TV. "We are so fucked." He pulled his own hair.

"Why?" Leslie asked. "What did you guys do? How do you know him?"

"Shut up," Sam said.

"If you don't tell me, I'll tell Mom and Dad." She took a few steps away from Sam.

She didn't need to say that she was mad because she was always left out. When we played football or wiffle ball with our friends or went to Joel's to hang out, she couldn't come. With the three kids, we were almost always paired off, never a true trio.

"Leslie, you really don't want to know," I said.

"I think I do," she said.

"His mom is a senator," Sam said.

"What?" I asked. I'd heard she was seeking reelection, but not for what. This was really fucking bad.

"You better tell me," Leslie said.

"A fucking senator," Sam said. "There's probably an army of cops looking for him. PIs everywhere. They probably have the security footage from Pilot last night."

"Officer Shelley knew our names," I said. She was going to tell them that she saw us last night.

Leslie screeched.

Sam and I both turned to her.

"If you do that one more time . . ." Sam clenched his fist.

"No, Sam," I said. Him hitting her wasn't going to make this any better. "Leslie, we're in trouble. Uncle Pauly and Joel, too. We're in big trouble. And if we tell you, you're going to be in trouble, too."

"I'm telling Mom and Dad and then there'll be *real* trouble." She took another step away from Sam.

Sam got up. I put a hand on his chest. He shoved me into the wall.

"Stop," I said. "Sam, this isn't going to—"

He wrenched my arm into a hammer lock. My shoulder roared with pain.

"Stop!" Leslie yelled.

But Sam was over the anger cliff, hurtling down now. He lifted me by the arm, and I thought my shoulder would tear before my face was hitting the floor. "You got us into this. You kept going into Uncle Pauly's room. You put the pictures online."

"What book? This is about a *book*?" Leslie asked.

"Don't you dare touch me," Sam said.

Leslie backed away from us.

"Stop!" I squealed.

His knee pinned my arm to my back. The pain was excruciating. Leslie ran up the stairs.

"Where is she going?" Sam asked.

"To get the book," I said, voice tight with pain.

"Fuck," he said, releasing my arm and scrambling after her.

Sam was faster than Leslie, but she had a head start. She cut the corner tight, pulling out of my sight as Sam hit the bottom of the stairs.

"Sam, stop," I said, but per usual, neither of them was listening to me. Him hitting Leslie was about the only way this could get worse. I shook my arm to help with the pain and chased them both.

Leslie got through the door as Sam hit the top of the second flight of stairs. I stopped at the bottom as she tried to slam the door. He managed to get his foot in. His bare foot.

SAY UNCLE

Sam howled. Leslie opened the door wide enough for him to fall backwards, then closed it. Sam writhed around, grabbing at his foot, a red line of bruise already forming. The lock clicked.

"Why didn't you do something?" Sam yelled at me.

"I tried to stop you. If you had any chill . . . "

"Then what?" His rocking was slowing, though he still rubbed his foot.

"We could have distracted her, or given her a different book, or done anything that wouldn't make the situation worse," I said. I rested my hands on my hips as I caught my breath.

Sam growled. I took two steps back, ready to run down the stairs and out the front door.

"Sam, you need to stay calm," I said, not because I thought anyone who has ever been told to stay calm has actually stayed calm, but because saying nothing might've been worse than saying something asinine.

The lock clicked again. The door swung in, and Leslie stepped out, holding the book in front of her. "Okay, seriously. What is this?"

CHAPTER 20

Away Message
Number1AvrilLavigneFanSoComplicated: My uncle needs emergency surgery and my brothers snuck out of the house. Can everyone just chill?

THE SIGHT OF the book in Leslie's hands froze Sam, which was good because if he hit me now I'd collapse.

Leslie brought the book down to the kitchen table with Sam limping after her. She pointed at a frog-like creature stretching down the side of a page next to what looked like a set of directions.

"What language is this?" Sam asked, pointing at some words in the impossible alphabet.

"Those are questions for Uncle Pauly," I said.

Leslie slammed the book shut. Sam jumped. "But what does this have to do with the missing man from TV?"

I opened my mouth, but Sam shushed me.

"If the police come and you know, they're going to torture you," he said. He had the people skills of a sledgehammer.

"Yeah right," Leslie said.

I scoffed. She'd tattled thousands of times. Sam and Braden won't let me play kickball. Sam and Braden didn't give me a turn on the TV. Sam and Braden stole the heads of my Barbie dolls and shaved their heads to use them as mini golf balls. As soon as Mom and Dad got home, I was sure she would snitch.

"Where did the man from the TV go?" Leslie asked. The screen reflected us back at ourselves.

"Look, Leslie—" I started.

Sam put up a hand to cut me off. "If you know, the police are going to come, and they're going to fill a bag with oranges and smash you with it. It's not going to leave any bruises."

"Leslie," I said, ignoring Sam's outstretched hands, "It's safer if you don't know."

She punched my arm. "Are you gonna go to jail?"

"Ow," I said, and rubbed the spot she hit.

"We don't know," I said, as Sam said, "Only if we get caught."

She looked back between us. "Braden, you can't leave me, too. Sam's already going away for college. I'm going to be stuck here alone with Mom and Dad."

I hugged her. Without looking up, she grabbed Sam's shirt and tugged him in, too. The three of us stood there like that until the phone rang. I was expecting Joel when I picked up the wireless handset, and it took me a moment to place the voice.

"Hello, is this the O'Riley residence?"

"Yes," I said.

"Braden," she said. I recognized her voice as Officer Shelley reintroduced herself, as if I could've forgotten last night. "Are your parents available?"

Sam was next to me, mouthing, "Who is it?" I waved him away.

I was already a little weepy from our group hug, and I willed myself to sound it. "No. They're at the hospital. With my uncle."

"I'm sorry to hear that, Braden," Officer Shelley said, voice void of emotion. "Do you know when they'll be back?"

"No," I said, and tried to force a sob, but even to me it sounded hollow. I mouthed the word "Shelley" to Sam. He slapped his thigh.

"Do you have a pen and paper? I'll need you to take a message for me."

"Right here," I said. She gave me her name (Brenda! She didn't look like a Brenda) and a number for my parents to call. I was too scared to ask what it was about.

She hung up. I left the note at Mom's place at the table. I dialed Joel's number.

Sam pressed my arm down. "What did she want?"

"For Mom and Dad to call when they get home," I said.

Sam grabbed his stomach. I picked the phone back up.

"The drug lady?" Leslie asked.

"Did she say about what?" he asked.

"I need to call Joel before she does," I said. I pressed the call button and the phone rang.

"Do you think she knows?" Sam asked.

"Knows what?" asked Leslie. She tugged on Sam's sleeve. "Is she going to question me, too?"

"You don't know anything, anyway," Sam said. He shoved her hand away.

Joel's mom picked up. "Braden, why the fuck do the police want to talk to Joel?"

"Hi, Mrs. Mancinas," I said.

"One, you know my last name is Flannagan and you can call me Carly." She took a deep breath, then yelled, "And two, why the fuck am I about to drive Joel to the police station?"

"I'm going to have to live here alone," Leslie said.

"Are Mom and Dad not people?" Sam asked.

I waved at them to shut up.

"Answer me, Braden," Ms. Flannagan said.

"Can I talk to Joel?" I asked.

"Abso-fucking-lutely not," she yelled. I held the phone back from my ear but could still hear her just fine. "Are you insane?"

"It's not Braden's fault," Joel said in the background.

"You know that's not what I mean," Leslie said. She punched Sam this time. She was too young for this.

SAY UNCLE

"Stop that," Sam said, but he looked like he wanted to punch someone, too.

"It's all a misunderstanding," I said to Joel's mom.

"What the fuck," Ms. Flannagan said. "I'm going to kill Joel, and then I'm going to kill you. You were supposed to be the good influence. What the fuck!" She hung up on me.

"Stop punching us!" Sam yelled.

Leslie rubbed her knuckles.

The phone rang again. This time, Ancy's name came up on the caller ID. For a second, my heart perked up. Was she calling to forgive me? To release me from my suffering? Then I remembered Uncle Pauly's plan. The orders from a dying man. My stomach turned over.

"Are you going to answer?" Leslie asked, dabbing her eyes.

I wondered if Ancy was hurting as badly as I was. Then I opened the door and walked outside. I could hear Sam yelling at me to tell him where I was going, not to leave him alone with all of this, but I kept going.

There was a small park with a softball field surrounded by woods at the end of our street. Leslie loved walking around, calling it a forest, though in reality it was too small for such a grand name. I made my way to the trail head, then walked along the path.

It followed a small stream, buzzing with mosquitos in the July heat. It didn't feel so hot under the canopy of leaves, the perfect place to hyperventilate.

It was all too much for me. Fifteen and being asked to cover up a murder. To accept that there was magic in the world. To seduce a girl and then sacrifice her to save my uncle's life. To find a replacement. I couldn't do it.

I grabbed a tree, focusing on the way the bark felt. The way the gray ridges formed a mosaic, almost like dragon scales before the moss turned them green. I wondered if the tree felt the moss, if it burned as it grew or if it was more like growing: something you don't feel, but one day you notice you're four inches taller.

Then, I screamed, loud as I could. I tried to yell the responsibilities away. I crouched, one hand still on the tree.

With my luck, a jogger was going to come by. Or some asshole walking their dog without a poop bag, and they'd ask me what was wrong. So I got up, legs shaky, and headed toward a basketball court on the other side of the river, glass from broken beer bottles glittering on the pavement.

Eventually, I'd have to go back, to face the tangle of my life, but for now I would stay in the park. And then I thought of Ancy, and how wonderful it would be to talk to her about this. To hold her hand, and to let all of this out. She'd comfort me, maybe run her hand through my hair. She'd take some of this weight off my shoulders.

CHAPTER 21

Away Message
EnterSamMan88: Deleting this stupid fucking
thing! No one talks to me on here anyways.

MOM AND DAD were home with Chinese food
when I returned from the woods. If I wasn't
around, it was the family go-to even though they
didn't have anything I'd eat on the menu. For every three
nights of Szechuan Wok, I managed to convince my
parents to have one night of pizza. At least Sam and Leslie
had the presence of mind to put the book away and shut
up about Screecher in the presence of our parents.

After exploding in the park, I was too numb to be mad
about it. I felt like a shell as I took a big helping of rice and
left the rest of the food.

My parents were tense, and I waited for them to bring
up Officer Shelley's call. But instead, Dad said, "Uncle
Pauly is going to be fine."

"Appendicitis," Mom said.

My mind flashed to Uncle Pauly telling me the magic
was attached to his appendix. Would having it removed
change anything?

"Four days before I married your mom, I started
having this intense pain in my side. I told Grandpa Clive
and he said, 'Sack up,'" Dad said. He pointed to the spot.
"But it kept getting worse. I kept telling him, and he kept
telling me to tough it out. So I did. Two days, and the pain
kept getting sharper. It felt like someone had impaled me.

113

So I went to the doctor. Two days before the wedding, I had the surgery. I could barely stand." Dad lifted his shirt to show us his scar.

"It's true. I had to hold him up during our first dance." Mom laughed.

"I'm telling you so you know that Uncle Pauly is going to be fine," he said. His shirt bunched as he tried to re-tuck it.

"Is Aunt Linda coming?" Leslie asked.

Mom and Dad exchanged a look.

"We're not sure," Mom said.

"I think she'd like to be there, but it's hard to take two kids on the train," Dad said.

No one addressed the cop out. The conversation moved on, and I waited for them to ask why the police were calling. Across the table from me, Sam kept shaking. He must've been as nervous as I was. The other shoe didn't drop, though.

Instead, they asked us about our days. No mention of Officer Shelley, Peter Schrader, or Uncle Pauly's book. Sam and Leslie must have gotten rid of the note.

Lunch that day felt like running through a gauntlet without getting hit.

After, Sam told me to come to his room.

"Why?"

He signaled for me to keep my voice down. "I got . . . "

"Officer Shelley knows that she talked to me. She's going to call again." For a genius, he sure was dumb.

"I was buying us time. But I have something else to tell you."

"Time for what?" I asked. He was glaring. If I wasn't careful, I was going to push him over his cliff, but I was getting close to mine, too. "What in God's name are we going to do between now and when Officer Shelley calls back tomorrow and Mom's home?"

"We can get to Joel and see what Officer Shelley asked him. I got . . . something. An email."

"About the book?" How had they gotten Sam's email?

"No. Something else," he said.

"I don't care about your girlfriend in Canada or whatever."

Sam shoved me. "If you want this to be a problem, I can make it a fucking problem."

"Get the phone."

"Do I look like your errand boy?"

"It's your plan."

Sam shoved me. I couldn't take another second looking at his stupid fucking face.

"Stop putting your dick in this," I said.

Sam shoved me again. This time, I braced. Then I pushed him back.

"Really, motherfucker?" he shouted.

Mom and Dad pounded up the stairs.

Sam came at me again. I sidestepped and locked him into a bear hug. He tried to pry my latched hands apart. I walked us toward his bed.

Dad came through the door. "Stop!"

Sam was a lot bigger than I was, so he probably didn't need the distraction to twist me around, throwing me. I landed half on his bed, my spine ramming into the frame.

Mom and Dad were yelling, but I didn't hear them. Sam pinned me against the bed frame, with one hand. He slapped me across the mouth with the other. I saw a flash of light. My lip cut against my teeth. That asshole.

I writhed to escape. There was another slap. I punched at his stomach. He didn't move.

The third time he closed his fist. My head rocked back against his mattress. A lump formed under my eye immediately.

Dad got between us. Mom was screeching in the corner.

"I'm going to call the police if you don't stop," Dad yelled.

That got Sam to stand up straight. I was still pinned, but the hitting had stopped. I shoved his hand away, and fell to the floor. The spot on my cheek where he'd punched me was tender to the touch.

"What's this about?" Dad asked.

"What happened?" Mom echoed.

"Sam's an asshole," I said.

Sam raised his hand again.

Dad backed him down. "You take Braden, I'll take Sam."

"All right, come on, Bray," Mom said.

She led me downstairs to her and Dad's room. The only places to sit were the bed or Dad's desk chair, and I didn't want to be next to her. I could tell it hurt her, but right then, I couldn't feel anyone's hurt but my own.

Mom folded her hands. "What did you do?"

"Oh, come on. He's older. Why is it my responsibility to keep him from kicking my ass?"

"Language."

"Really? That's the problem here?" I asked. Dad's chair rolled when I waved my hand.

"You know how Sam is," Mom said, rubbing her leg.

"Isn't he supposed to be taking care of me?"

Mom sighed. "Braden, you keep telling us that you're fifteen, and that means you're almost an adult, but you're not acting like it."

"Are you serious? You don't even know what happened, and you're going to say that it's my fault?"

"I'm not here to assign blame. I'm here to talk about how we can prevent this from happening in the future." Mom smoothed out a wrinkle on the bedspread.

"Okay. How about this for an idea: Don't give away my room and make me sleep on Sam's floor all summer."

"When you're older, you'll understand. I would do anything for my brother, and you should, too." She couldn't make eye contact as she spoke.

"Oh really?" I squeezed the arm rests of the chair.

"Yes, Braden. Really."

"What if I saw Uncle Pauly kill a man last night and helped him hide the car? What if Sam and Joel were there, too? Are you going to cover up the murder?"

The air conditioner behind me cycled off as part of its Money Saver mode. The room shifted as a layer of heat and humidity siphoned in.

Mom shook her head and told me not to tell fairy tales. "If that were true, I'd do anything for my brother. If he killed someone, he had a good reason."

"And what would you want me to do?" I asked. She never believed me.

Now she looked me right in the eye. She held herself like she'd just finished a marathon, shoulders slumped. "Everything we do is for our family. It's the most important thing."

"Can this conversation be over?" I fell back in the chair. It rolled into Dad's desk.

"No," she said. "I need to know what happened with you and Sam. He's your family. You only get one."

"He's a fucking psycho and I stood up to him."

"Language!"

"Is that all that matters to you? That I don't swear or do anything that might embarrass you? You know people are going to ask about this bruise, right?" My cheek throbbed, as if in acknowledgement of what I'd said.

"Braden, of course your feelings matter to me. But if you ever want to get ahead in life, you're going to have to stop swearing. You're going to need to protect your family. Sam might be mad right now, but he'd do anything for you, don't you see that? If you were in trouble, your brother would be there."

"He *is* the trouble. Someone needs to protect me from him!"

"I don't understand where all of this anger and bitterness is coming from." She folded her arms.

"You forced me to go to an all-boys high school I don't

want to go to, you gave away my bedroom, and when Sam hits me you don't do anything." My cheek was tender as I wiped away a tear. "You're going to punish us both like you always do, like it's my fault that he uses me as a punching bag when he loses his temper."

"Braden, I love you, but I'm very disappointed in you right now." She held out a tissue box for me.

I slapped it away.

Mom sighed. "Your brother is going through a hard time."

"How?" I asked, though he had been next to me when Uncle Pauly killed Screecher. That scene probably echoed in his head as it did in mine.

She looked down. "He got waitlisted at Princeton."

"How? There's no mail on Sunday," I said.

"He signed up for email. He wanted to know as soon as possible. They told him Friday."

My first thought was that Sam would get into a hundred other schools. But then I considered the hours he'd spent studying, the effort he'd dedicated to Princeton over the last three years. "That sucks."

Mom sighed. "Braden, you're old enough to know. Your brother is sick."

"Sick?" I asked, and imagined the worst: cancer.

"Mentally." She shook her head, unable to make eye contact with me.

"Depression? Anxiety? Bipolar?"

"That's private. All you need to know is that your brother is sick, and we need you to take some responsibility. It's hurting all of us."

"You're not the one with a black eye right now." Did she believe what she was saying?

She stood up and waited a second, to see if I had anything else to say.

It was time wasted.

"Stay here," she said, leaving me to await my punishment while she and Dad convened.

SAY UNCLE

They came back with our punishments. Sam was going to lose the Xbox for a week, which meant that I was losing my Xbox privilege too as it sat in Dad's trunk. My phone privileges were gone. I didn't know and I didn't care how they were going to try to enforce that. They weren't home all day and it wasn't like they could take the phone off the hook.

They left Sam and me to sit in his room.

"Sorry," Sam said. He was back, anger safely passed.

"It's okay," I said, even though it wasn't.

"It's not." Sam was sitting on his bed, staring at his hands.

"Sam, we need to figure out what Joel said to Officer Shelley before she calls again. Mom and Dad are going to kill us."

"I don't know what happened." He rubbed at the bruises on his knuckle.

"Maybe we can sneak out, see Joel in person. His mom isn't going to let him talk to me after our last phone call."

"I don't want to hurt anybody."

"But Joel is cool. He's not blabbing."

"I love you, Braden."

"Is there any reason we'd be suspects?" I heard what Sam was saying. I had heard it every time he said it.

"I love you," he said, more forcefully this time.

"I love you too, and I'm sorry you got waitlisted. But, we tried to hide a missing person's car last night. After we saw him get murdered. Or whatever the hell that was."

"I know. It's all so fucked."

"We need to get to Joel."

"I'll get the phone," Sam said.

The phone rang twice before Joel's mom picked up. "Braden, he's grounded. And you're lucky I'm not calling your parents. Call again in two weeks." Then she hung up.

CHAPTER 22

Away Message
bigRican787: This is Joel's mom. He's grounded. He'll answer your messages when he gets his computer privileges back.

WE WAITED FOR our parents to go to bed, then snuck out. Leslie's window was a story up from the garage's roof.

"Where are you going?" Leslie asked in an obnoxious stage whisper. "Does this have to do with the book?"

Sam started, "This has to do with—"

But I cut him off. "We'll do your chores for a week. We'll be back in an hour. But you can't say anything."

Leslie liked that.

"I'm not doing any extra chores," Sam said.

I wanted to say, "When do you do your regular ones?" but I didn't want another fight.

We slinked out the window onto the garage, then lowered ourselves onto the soft grass of the backyard. To avoid the noise of the engine igniting and the empty space in the driveway, we walked up to Joel's.

We moved in silence. This was the last part of Sam's cycle. There was an explosion, an apology, and then absolute quiet. It was unsettling, the peace of a gun being reloaded during a shootout. Who knew when he'd explode again.

The streets between our house and Joel's were quiet, but we cut through the woods the same way we had the night before, anyway. Neither of us wanted to confront the street where Uncle Pauly killed Screecher. Still, my mind wandered to it, wondering if the spot was still cold like Joel had said, or if the day's heat had warmed it.

Joel's room faced the back of the house and the light was on. But so was the light directly below it: his mother's room.

Sam and I crouched, waiting for Joel's mom to go to sleep, but she wasn't like our parents, who went to bed around 10 every evening.

"Ring the doorbell," Sam said.

"And say what? She won't even let me talk to Joel on the phone." I shooed a mosquito off my arm.

"Don't say anything. Ring it, then run back here." Sam scooped up a handful of pebbles. "I'll throw these at Joel's window while she's checking who's at the door."

"What if Joel answers?" I asked.

"Do you think Joel answers the door at his house?"

Fair point.

I edged alongside the house, back against the wall, headed for the front door. I kept thinking that the worst-case scenario was Ms. Flannagan catching me. Then she'd call my parents, and they'd know about Officer Shelley. Which, as far as worst-case scenarios went, was pretty fucking bad. But she wasn't going to bed anytime soon and the mosquitoes were biting.

The lamp above their stoop was off, flanked by unlit windows on either side. I rang the bell five or ten times in a row then booked it toward the woods behind the house.

The porch lamp came on as I turned the corner around the side of the house. I leaned against the wall again and waited, out of breath.

"Real funny," Ms. Flannagan yelled from the steps. "Is that you, Braden?"

Shit. Who else would be ringing their doorbell at 10 at night?

Her slippers echoed down the steps. She was coming

around the side of the house to check. I sprinted past Sam, who was throwing another pebble at Joel's window.

"C'mon," I half-whispered, half-yelled.

Sam turned, then he must've seen Ms. Flannagan because he double-timed it back into the woods.

The two of us collapsed. "Did she see us?" I whispered.

"I don't know," Sam said, panting.

"Braden?" Ms. Flannagan called out again. "If you come out now, I won't tell your parents."

A flashlight cut above us in the woods.

"Did Joel see you?" I asked.

"Yeah," Sam said.

"Then why were you throwing more rocks?"

"Braden," Ms. Flannagan called again. Her flashlight swept through the woods, slower this time, focused on the ground. It was coming straight for us. All we could do was stand up and surrender.

Then Joel yelled, "Mom, the Turner kids are in the sideyard again."

The light stopped. "Oh those little fucks." Ms. Flannagan ran back toward the steps.

Sam and I got up. Joel came to the window and signaled for us to give him five minutes.

We stayed low as we waited, watching for Joel at the backdoor. We didn't see him coming up behind us from the other side.

"What's up, boys?"

Sam jumped.

"How the hell—?" I choked out, heart pounding.

He dapped us both, not acknowledging our surprise.

"What happened?" Sam asked. "With Officer Shelley?"

"I've only got like two minutes. Everything was about the people we saw that night," he said. "And if we noticed the car."

SAY UNCLE

"So we're not suspects?" I asked.

Joel raised his eyebrows. "Dude, we're kids to them. And they don't think you guys could steal someone's lunch money. The only thing you kill are the curves on tests, nerds."

So at least one thing had gone well. I was ready to go home and sleep for another month when Sam asked, "So why did your mom ground you?"

"She said I shouldn't be hanging around anywhere the police need to question anybody, she said, 'You don't know who's going to say you did it.'" His voice falsettoed as he mimicked her.

Sam was staring at Joel, disbelieving. But I knew my best friend. We could trust him.

"He asked me—"

"Joel?" his mom yelled from the front door. "Where the hell did he go?"

"You gotta get back," Sam said.

"Yo. What the fuck happened with your uncle last night?" Joel said, his voice lower, his facade cracking.

"I don't know," I said.

"He saved us," Sam said.

"I've been . . . not doing great," Joel said.

"Me too," I said.

"You want to get grounded for double?" Joel's mom yelled.

I'd heard Sam crying the night before, but tonight he said, "Go. Forget about it. We get through the police, we get Uncle Pauly better, and everything will be okay."

I don't know if he even believed it.

CHAPTER 23

Away Message
BrayDay327: Stomach is sick. I wish the rock would squash me against the hard place.

MY PELVIS PRESSED against the hardwood floor through the near-empty air mattress, but I was too tired to do anything about it. Face down, I fell asleep before Sam returned from brushing his teeth. Maybe he wanted to talk, but it would've taken a defibrillator to wake me.

The dream started like the last. Paul Jr. showed me through the closet, leading me into the room. I tried to put on the brakes, but again, I was a passenger in my body. I had no control.

Paul Jr., eyes vacant, opened the door, pushing me off into the room with the cornucopia, the miasma of moss and decay. I struggled to break free of the paralysis, to no avail. Screecher's intestines hung out of the mouth of the cornucopia. Something cast a shadow over it.

The floor creaked as a black robed figure stepped onto the altar. It turned toward me, face enveloped in darkness. It took off its hood. Uncle Pauly.

He looked slimmer, like he'd been hitting the gym twice a day; he stood taller, like the pain in his knees had vanished.

"You know what you need to do." He slipped the skull knife out of his pocket.

I shook my head.

SAY UNCLE

"I killed for you." He circled the altar, scraping the blade along it. Sparks flew from the edge and an image wafted up. Screecher, with his tendrils of energy wrapped around Uncle Pauly. Joel's ax hits Screecher. Uncle Pauly's hand goes down the throat, and then again, he pulls Screecher inside out like a handbag.

Joel's cheering didn't break the tension this time. I was watching a man die.

Something in the back of the room rustled.

Uncle Pauly opened his robe. His skin was gone. His organs pulsated, bulging into each other, nothing like the cleanly separated diagrams from my biology book. He touched a darker tube that wrapped around his appendix. "The poison is here."

As if attached to his finger, a mist of sickly green sprayed out. It hovered in front of him like a fog. "The doctors will take out the organ, but this is going to spread. To my heart. To my lungs. My kidneys. Everywhere.

"Don't let me down."

Screecher's death replayed on the altar again.

"Only blood pays for blood. Death for death."

Still, I was paralyzed.

Uncle Pauly closed his robe, organs thankfully concealed. He stepped back into the shadows. The thing back there with him swished. I tensed, waiting to see if it was going to come forward. If it had something to add, hoping against all hopes that I wouldn't need to look at it. Smelling it was enough.

Something touched my hand. If I had control of my body, I would've screamed. The Paul Jr. shell held my hand, guiding me out, back to the waking world. We passed through the dark closet silently.

I woke up exhausted. The clock on Sam's bedside table, identical to the one in my room, glowed 3am. Sam snored quietly in bed. I took Uncle Pauly's directions from my pillowcase and ran my finger over the lip of the envelope.

I didn't know if I should read the instructions or tear them into a thousand pieces and flush them down the toilet.

I fought sleep until 4. Then I shoved the envelope back into the pillowcase and surrendered to a black, dreamless night.

When I woke again, Sam was snoring loudly. I whispered his name twice to be sure, and then I opened the envelope. The instructions started out simple. Directions for buying a Metrocard and which subway to ride from Grand Central to Uncle Pauly's. What was good at the restaurant downstairs. Uncle Pauly even put in two-hundred bucks so I could treat Ancy to her final meal.

Take her to the room with the dagger.

The room I couldn't escape in my dreams. I was supposed to chain her down, and then read from the book.

"What are you moping about?" Leslie asked. She'd come in without knocking. I stuffed the paper back in the envelope. Mom and Dad really needed to reevaluate their "no lock" policy.

"I'm not moping. And can't you see Sam is sleeping?"

"Fine," she said. She turned to leave.

I followed her and asked, "Would you do something Uncle Pauly told you to do, even if you thought it was bad?"

She stopped in the doorway. "Dude, he's getting divorced because he treats Aunt Linda so badly." She left for real this time. When I thought things couldn't get worse, I got schooled by my eleven-year-old sister.

My stomach ached as I nibbled at a bowl of dry Cheerios, alone at the table. The phone, now a banned object, rang. The police station came up on the caller ID. Great. I got up, paused to see if the pain in my stomach would break, and then wandered listlessly toward the TV.

Mom ran down the stairs, trying to catch the call before it went to the answering machine. "Braden, answer the phone!"

I shuffled along. "I'm not allowed." Without thinking about it, I ran my finger along the edge of the bruise on my cheek, confirming it did indeed still hurt.

I didn't want to be in the room when Officer Shelley told Mom that we were needed for questioning in relation to a missing persons case, but there was nowhere else to go. In a house full of six people, it was impossible to be alone.

"Hello," Mom said. "Yes, this is she."

I was the Roadrunner the moment he realizes that he's left the ground, that gravity is about to smash him to bits.

"May I ask what this is in regards to? I didn't receive a message."

Other parents would lie, and say they'd been too busy to call. Maybe they'd throw their kids under the bus, or take up for them. My mom was like Sam, though, brilliant memory but very little understanding of what was happening around her emotionally.

"Oh," Mom said. She covered her mouth with her hand.

I closed my eyes, trying to squeeze them tight enough that the exhaustion would pass. The phone privilege was only going to be the beginning at home. It would be worse when the police found out what we'd seen. What we'd done.

"Of course. Yes. Sam and Braden will be there in fifteen minutes." Then to me, "Braden, wake your brother. Now."

Today couldn't get any better.

CHAPTER 24

Away Message
Number1AvrilLavigneFanSoComplicated:
What happens when the people you love
most go away?

THE MILFORD POLICE STATION was across from the hardware store in the center of town. A black officer in street blues walked us back to a questioning room with a window overlooking Ancy's work. The chairs had plastic backs, and Sam and I instinctively sat at the ones facing the door, but I twisted 180 degrees toward the window to figure out if she was working.

Maybe afterward I could walk over. It had been three days. I know that it might be hard to believe at this point, but I wasn't thinking about Uncle Pauly's bargain. I liked her and I missed her. I wanted to see her.

Sam kept fidgeting. "What are you going to say if they ask about your black eye?"

The bruise was more on my cheek, but being pedantic might've gotten me another. "I'll say I fell down the stairs."

"Don't. They'll know."

He looked clammy, like he hadn't slept, either.

"Then what do you want me to say?"

"Say you fell off your bike." He rubbed his bruised knuckles.

"And got a bruise on my cheek but nowhere else? Wouldn't I scrape up my elbows and wrists if I really fell off my bike?"

128

SAY UNCLE

"You can't say I hit you." He was really sweating it. "I'm only here because I was looking out for you."

I was insulted that he was asking. Sure, we had our problems, but I wasn't going to call the police. I felt embarrassed for Dad when he threatened to.

Officer Shelley knocked on the door as she opened it in one motion, startling both of us. "Hi again, boys."

She flipped a chair backwards, and straddled it. She slapped a file folder on the table in front of her. "Did your mother tell you why you were here?"

Both of us shook our heads. She hadn't, and I didn't want to offer that we'd already talked to Joel. I didn't know the rules, but it seemed like discussing a police interview with another witness would be frowned upon.

She slapped a headshot of Screecher from the folder on the center of the table.

I tried not to flinch.

"This man, Peter Schrader, went missing on Saturday night. Have you seen anything about him on the news?"

We nodded.

"He's the senator from New Jersey's son, right?" I asked.

Officer Shelley slid his photo over to us. "Mr. Schrader's car was tracked to the parking lot at the Pilot by a private investigator early Sunday morning. They're not sure what business he had in Milford. Did you see Mr. Schrader on the evening in question?"

I made a point of squinting at the photo, really combing through it. My mind replayed Uncle Pauly's hand going down his throat, his insides falling outside of his body. I focused on keeping my face straight, not trembling, being the clueless dipshit Officer Shelley thought I was.

"I didn't see him," I said.

Officer Shelley turned toward Sam. "What about you?"

"Never seen him before," Sam said.

She covered Screecher's photo with one of his car taken

129

from the front. "What about this vehicle?" She flanked it with pictures from the side and with the license plate.

Again, I studied the pictures without focusing my eyes. Part of me thought that maybe I could see if Joel left any fingerprints. Logically that might've been the stupidest thing I'd ever thought.

"No," I said.

"I saw where it was parked on the news," Sam said. "We were on the other side of the building. We had to get close to the door to get Uncle Pauly in."

Officer Shelley nodded. "That's something else I need to ask you about. Do you have a good phone number for your uncle?"

"Of course," Sam said. "But he had an appendectomy last night, so I don't know how much of a help he'll be. We thought he'd had too much to drink, but it was much worse."

Officer Shelley pursed her lips. She had something to say, but she kept it to herself.

"Did you see anyone..." she started. "Did you notice anyone suspicious?"

At the Pilot, everyone was suspicious. Stoners and long-distance truckers. I couldn't exactly say that to Officer Shelley, though.

"No. Did you?"

Sam shook his head.

"Okay. I was there, too. I saw the usual crowd, but I was hoping your ears were closer to the ground," Officer Shelley said. She gathered up her photos. "If you boys think of anything else, call me right away. They think Mr. Schrader may still be alive—"

Sam gagged.

"Are you all right?" Officer Shelley asked.

Sam grabbed a trash can from the corner. He unleashed into it, probably not noticing that it was unlined.

"He's nervous about being questioned," I said. I rubbed his back, trying to make this look like a regular event. "He threw up at the SATs, too."

SAY UNCLE

Sam wretched again. From the smell, I could tell it was the worst kind of puke: all bile.

"And you're sure you didn't see anything?"

I avoided Officer Shelley's gaze. The window framed Ancy taking down hanging plants in front of the hardware store. She reached the wire they hung on easily, but she strained under the weight of them.

"No," Sam said, pulling his head out from the trash can. "It's just my nervous stomach."

Whether Officer Shelley believed us or not, she let us go without any more questions.

We stepped out into the sun, heat blasting into the 80s. Across the street, Ancy hosed the plants she'd lined up on the sidewalk. She squinted against the glare, head pointed in our direction. I hoped that she'd wave, that she'd forgiven me.

Sam nudged me. "Is that her? Are you going to say hi?"

Mom shepherded us toward the car. "I can't believe I had to take you to the police station on the day of your uncle's surgery."

"Yeah," I said. "Wait a minute." I broke from them and jogged across the street. If I'd thought about it more, I would've left her alone. But in my head, Uncle Pauly's dream-voice echoed, *blood for blood*.

"No way," Mom said.

"Mom, give him a second," Sam said, voice trailing.

Ancy definitely saw me now. She struggled to hold a smile down. Water leaked out from the bottom of the plants, tributaries from each pot meeting in a stream at the edge of the sidewalk. A customer hopscotched through them.

"Hi," I said. I wasn't sure if I should kiss her or hug her or stop and wave, but I thought about what Uncle Pauly would do. It was all about confidence. So I kissed her unpuckered lips like it was the most natural thing in the world.

"Wow," she said, pulling away. "I didn't expect that after not hearing from you since Saturday."

"I know," I said. I blushed and cursed my inability to stop it. It felt so good to see her, and the waiting seemed so stupid now. "I lost my phone privilege."

"Oh my God," she said. "What happened to your cheek?"

I rubbed the bruise where Sam had clobbered me. "My brother. And I'm the one who lost my phone privilege."

"They let him hit you like that?" Water from the hose nozzle dripped onto her jeans.

"That's not the half of it. Uncle Pauly's getting an appendectomy."

"Are you okay?" Ancy rubbed my arm, her touch beyond gentle.

The water from the plants seeped onto my shoes. I thought about what Uncle Pauly had asked me to do to her. I saw Screecher turning inside out. Another customer walked into the store, ringing the bell at the top of the door.

I couldn't, but I had to. *Death for death.*

I'm not sure how long I stared into nothing before Ancy said, "Braden?"

"Yeah, yeah. He'll be fine."

"That's good," she said. The sun beat down on us as midday approached. "I'm going to have to get back to work."

The words Uncle Pauly instructed me to say ran through my head on a ticker. *Come to New York with me. I know a great spot to grab appetizers, right below my uncle's apartment.* The words tickled the tip of my tongue. Uncle Pauly said I owed him. Mom said that I should do anything for my family. But Ancy was in front of me, upset that I hadn't called her. I didn't love her, we'd gone on two dates, but I knew in that moment that Uncle Pauly was wrong about everything and I rejected his games and the sacrifice. "You need to watch out. My uncle Pauly, he's after you."

"What?" she said, jaw hanging down.

"Ancy," her manager called from inside the store. "Send your friend away."

"Stay away from him," I said, and jogged away as she went inside.

I had asked Uncle Pauly for help with Screecher, not to get himself into a magic tangle. It didn't matter what he said. If we had to sacrifice someone, it wouldn't be Ancy.

CHAPTER 25

Away Message
FancyAncy89: Boys are the worst.

WHEN WE GOT HOME. Mom went to her room, silent. Normally when she was mad she'd do chores loudly, cursing under her breath. This, leaving us without a single sound was new and scary.

Sam turned on the TV downstairs, and I plopped onto the husk of the air mattress upstairs. I closed my eyes for all of three seconds before the phone rang.

Sam came in shortly after. "Joel called. Mom wouldn't let me bring the phone up, but she didn't stop me from talking to him."

When I rolled over on the air mattress to look at him, my knee cracked against the floor.

"Even though he took the post down, he's still getting emails," Sam said. "He got one from the private investigator that's looking into Screecher's disappearance. He wants to 'chat' with Joel."

"Oh fuck." This had to be more sorcerer shit. I couldn't breathe. "They're cutting out the police."

"Joel said he's coming over."

"Isn't he grounded?"

"His mom's at work and he full-screened his grandpa's computer on porn and his grandpa is freaking out because he doesn't know how to close it."

⊸

SAY UNCLE

Mom was sitting at the kitchen table with the phone in front of her. She stopped us with a look. "Where do you think you're going?"

"Any news on Uncle Pauly's surgery?" Sam asked.

Mom glanced at the phone and shook her head.

Sam rubbed her back. "It's all going to be okay, Mom."

"Am I going to be taking you to the police station again?" She batted his hand away.

"No," I said.

"I try to do everything right," she said. "You're at church every Sunday. We pay for you to go to a school that's in line with our values. But then on a Monday morning in the middle of the summer, I get a call to bring you in for questioning."

A pit of guilt solidified in my stomach. "It's not your fault, Mom."

"We were witnesses," Sam said. "Not criminals."

"I've been a good mother to you, haven't I?"

"Yes," I said.

"Of course," Sam added.

"Then why are you breaking my heart?" she asked. "Why are you leaving again as your uncle has surgery? What are people going to say, while he's on the operating table you're getting questioned by the police? Then going to Joel's for a swim like nothing happened?"

"We wouldn't be going if it wasn't important." My fingernails dug into my palm. I wanted to scream at her.

"What could possibly be as important as your uncle's surgery?" She leaned back from the table.

"This is to help him," I said, knowing she wouldn't believe me. She never believed me.

"You're helping your uncle Pauly by what, smoking a joint with Joel? Everyone knows about him," she said, as if half the kids our age in the city weren't smoking.

Sam ducked out of Mom's line-of-sight.

"I don't smoke," I said. "Even if he does."

"Who's going to believe that? Even if you're telling the truth, what's it going to look like when you're applying for college? 'Spent summers smoking pot with townie neighbor.'" She looked at the phone, as if she could will it to ring.

"Joel is my best friend," I said.

"That's the problem. Your father doesn't think we should say anything. He says that you'll grow out of it, that you'll find more fitting friends at Precious Blood and your old friends will naturally fall away, but now you're being questioned by the police. What do you think the other kids at your school are doing?"

"I didn't even want to go there," I said. "And half of their dads are in the mob." Another truth she'd never accept.

"Don't be ridiculous."

The doorbell rang.

"Tell Joel to leave," Mom said. "Your uncle's having surgery. If you think losing the phone for a week is bad . . . "

"No," I said.

Sam took a step farther from me, like my rebellion was an infectious disease.

"Fine." The vortex of her anger sucked the rest of the feeling out of the room.

I opened the door. "Hey dude," I said, quietly.

Joel came in. "Hi, Mrs. O'Riley. How are you?"

Mom didn't answer.

I steered Joel out to the backyard. A covered grill flanked a patio table set with peeling white paint. Sam stayed with Mom. If I were him, I would've done the same thing.

"Dude, I didn't think she could get angry." His chair dragged across the patio as he pulled it out.

"I've never seen her like this before. She's really mad about the police station thing." I leaned my elbows on the table across from him.

"My mom, too."

"Trust me, I know."

"What are we going to do about this private investigator? Is your uncle still in the hospital?" Joel picked at his cast.

"He's still in surgery," I said. The grates of the table pressed pink diamond indentations into my arm.

"The guy said he's coming to my house at 3," Joel said.

"Did he say what he wanted?" I asked.

"He isn't going to the police. He must want the book," Joel said. Dark rings raccooned his eyes. Screecher had threatened to kill Joel's family and he'd ended up sloshing organs on the pavement. But who was going to stop the second investigator?

Something clicked in my head, and I knew I had to tell him. "Uncle Pauly wants me to sacrifice Ancy to this thing in his apartment in New York."

"What the fuck."

"I almost asked her to go to the city when I saw her today."

"What the fuck, dude!" Joel waved his hands wildly as he spoke. "What's wrong with you? You've got a sister and a mother, and even if you didn't, just like, what the fuck."

I couldn't look at him. "I warned her instead. It's all coming together, though. We can feed the thing someone else."

Joel frowned. "Is Uncle Pauly planning to blood sacrifice me, too? Feed this thing all of the brown people?"

"We're Mexican," I said.

"You're the color of chalk."

Which was true, but this was all beside the point. "The private investigator. We can catch him and sacrifice him. Whoever he is, he's not an innocent."

"The last guy had magic ropes, like some Wonder Woman shit. And we can't just kill people," Joel said.

"It's either we do this or Uncle Pauly dies. I don't know anyone with more knives than you."

He slammed a butterfly knife on the table. "What's this going to do against a magic rope?"

"We owe Uncle Pauly and we can't give it Ancy," I said.

Joel flicked the knife open and then closed. "It's wrong."

He had caught his hand in between the blade and handle of that knife at least three times in front of me. But what other option did we have? "If Uncle Pauly dies, it'll be our fault. That's wrong, too."

He sighed. "Will it? We didn't bring that book to your house. We didn't do a piss poor job of hiding it. And I'm supposed to help you kill someone because of it?"

"Screecher said he was going to kill your family. You think the person they send after him won't?"

"Who is 'they'? You sound fucking crazy right now. I don't want to kill anyone and I'm not going to help you do it."

"Just go home. Have fun with your new private investigator friend."

"Give me the book," Joel said. "We get rid of that, and these fucking whackos stop coming to my house. Maybe you can stop coming to my house, too."

"Fuck you, dude," I said. I stood and shoved him even though he had a hundred pounds on me. He didn't budge.

"I'm not going to kick your ass because your uncle is in surgery and you fucked it up with your girlfriend," he said.

I turned away from him so he wouldn't see the tears welling in my eyes. "Just go. Fuck off."

"So I don't do your plan and now you let some fucking magic asshole kill me? What a great friend you are."

CHAPTER 26

Away Message
BrayDay327: Everything is horrible.

WHEN I CAME INSIDE, Mom was there to hug me. I stiffened, unable to reconcile the embrace with how mad she'd been twenty minutes earlier. At first, I thought she'd been listening, that she'd realized I was on the verge of crying.

Then she said, sobbing, "The surgery didn't go well."

For a second, I wondered if he was dead, if I would be relieved of what he was asking me to do. I knew I should've felt like a piece of shit for thinking that, but I didn't. And even now, I don't. I wouldn't wish death on my own uncle, but it would've stopped a lot of bad things from happening.

"It wasn't his appendix. They don't know—what's wrong." She took deep breaths between sentences. "Uncle Pauly—" she sobbed, "—is in recovery. And we're going to— see him."

Dad was at work, so Sam read the printed Mapquest directions to Mom, the price of riding shotgun. Leslie flipped the pages of a *Baby-Sitters Club* book, eyes unfocused. I let it all soak around me. A moment of normalcy was a balm for chaos.

If I could grab the new investigator without Joel, I could be a regular teenager again. Maybe I could get Ancy an "I love New York" t-shirt. I was so hopelessly stupid.

Uncle Pauly was recovering on the fourth floor, in a bed too small for his body. He'd sprouted a layer of stubble. The various machines he was hooked to beeped discordant harmonies. His unfocused eyes wandered across the four of us. "Family. How are you?"

We all answered with variations of "good" at once. Mom rushed to his bedside, hugging her brother.

Leslie walked over to the bed and stared at the place the bandage stuck out under Uncle Pauly's hospital gown. "Does it hurt?"

"It's a minor surgery." His booming voice was a wisp of its former self. "Like getting hit by a compact car instead of a truck." He turned to me. "Are you set for your trip tomorrow?"

Sam and I stood awkwardly at the foot of the bed. The room was too small for us to go anywhere else. "Not the way you think. But yes," I said.

"What trip, Braden?" Mom's eyebrows nearly shot off the top of her head.

"Let him go, Ana. If you hold him too tight, he'll never fly home."

"That's the painkillers talking." Mom turned to me. "You're not going anywhere tomorrow, Braden."

"I'll chaperone," Sam said, again making things worse without realizing it.

"He's got to go . . . " Uncle Pauly's voice faded. Then his eyes fluttered shut.

The machines wired to Uncle Pauly beeped steadily.

"Pauly, your blood pressure and heart beat aren't changing. I know you didn't pass out."

He opened his eyes. "Shit, well, you've got to let the kid go."

"Where?"

"He's doing me a favor, in the city."

"You want me to let my fifteen-year-old go into New York City by himself, to do what exactly?" She backed away from the bed. Her lower lip quivered.

SAY UNCLE

He couldn't exactly say, but if one of us was going to lie to her, let it be him. She couldn't take away any of his privileges.

"Braden and Sam are going in to pick up something important for me." Uncle Pauly closed his eyes again.

"Do we need to do this now?" Mom seemed about to burst with tears. "Sam is only seventeen. My sons are not taking the train into New York City by themselves."

We kids butted out so the adults could fight.

"We used to."

"Mom, also put us on a plane to Mexico by ourselves when I was *nine*."

"And we were fine."

Mom shook her head. "C'mon, kids. We're leaving. He's delirious."

Uncle Pauly kept on talking, but Mom was power walking down that corridor and we had to jog to keep up.

When we got home, Mom went into the garage and took the front tire off my bike. She carried it inside. She didn't say anything, but she made sure I saw. Message received. I grabbed the camera.

"I've got feet," I said out of earshot, and walked toward Joel's. I was pissed at him, but I'd fix it after I took care of the new whacko. That thought brought me to Screecher and I wanted to cry or throw up, anything to get that feeling out. But I couldn't let Uncle Pauly die. And I couldn't let someone kill Joel no matter how pissed at him I was.

I cut through the woods and lay there to wait, watching each car and wondering if this was the one. I didn't know what to expect from the "private investigator," but I figured a few pictures of the guy would make a nice insurance policy.

I watched traffic through the camera's viewfinder for a while. Joel's street was quiet, a suburban fantasy. Two-

141

story houses with yards stretching into one another. Somewhere someone splashed in a pool. No breeze broke the heat. One of Joel's neighbors walked down the street with her dog. The animal turned in my direction, but the human didn't.

I wasn't exactly sure how I'd subdue the investigator. I watched a lot of action movies, and the heroes in them always seemed to knock out the bad guys with one punch. But I'd played punch-for-punch in the woods with Joel, whaling on each other's arms, and neither of had ever conked out, so that wouldn't work. I dug around and found a rock that I could clock them with and lay back down.

The envelope pressed against my leg pocket. I felt like shit for even thinking about asking Ancy. But I'd done the right thing. I'd warned her and she'd be safe now. This private investigator, not so much, but he used magic. He assumed this risk.

I was deep in thought when someone tapped my shoulder.

"Roll over," a high-pitched voice said.

I obeyed.

A woman in a black sweater and tan pants towered over me. She wore her blonde hair in a bun. She pointed to the camera. "What are you holding?"

"A camera."

"Nothing tricked out about it? It's not going to shoot a demon in my face?" She didn't have any weapon I could see, but I remembered those tendrils coming out of Screecher.

"No."

"Put it down, and then roll twice away from it."

She looked ready to kill. I did what she said.

She knelt down next to me. "Now empty your pockets."

I piled everything but the envelope with Uncle Pauly's directions—wallet with my newly-acquired debit card and maybe $50 in cash, house keys, clean pocket tissues, used ones, tic tacs—to my right.

"Is that all?" She poked at my possessions with a stick. "Nothing that's going to hurt me?"

"There's a pocket knife on my keychain."

"What are you hiding?" I swallowed hard, trying to think of something to distract her. Her eyes drilled into mine. Lying to her would be like grabbing a viper by the tail.

I took out the envelope.

"Whoa," she said. "Put it down."

I did. She prodded it away from me with her stick. "You're young. It took Screech years to become an asshole." She lifted the envelope half off the ground so she could read the front, but there hadn't been any writing. Then she muttered something that sounded like what Uncle Pauly had said before he killed Screecher. Letters like the ones in the book appeared on the front of the envelope. She let it drop down into the dirt.

"I'm guessing that you didn't write this. That right, kid?"

"Yes." I swallowed. If she could speak that language, she could turn me inside out.

"Who wrote it?"

I propped myself up on my elbows so I could die sitting up. "I can't tell you."

"What's your name?"

"Joel."

She rolled her eyes. "Your actual name."

"Braden."

"You're protecting whoever wrote that, huh, Braden?"

I nodded.

"Did that someone have anything to do with Schrader disappearing?"

"I plead the Fifth."

"Kid, you're starting to piss me off."

I didn't say anything. It was hot, but that wasn't why I was sweating.

"I'm going to give you one more chance." She cracked

her knuckles. "You tell me, or I reach into your little brain and take out what I need to know. It'll hurt. And you'll deserve it."

I was going to regret this, either way, but Uncle Pauly had saved Joel's family. Uncle Pauly *was* family. I couldn't give him up. "No."

"Braden." She sighed. "Last chance. Either you help me willingly, pain free, or you help me unwillingly. That's going to hurt a whole lot. There's a chance you'll hemorrhage."

I don't know how but she made me imagine my nose bursting with blood, soaking the front of my shirt. I pictured red leaking out of my ears and eyes and mouth and the tiny pores in my skin.

"Five."

She grabbed my forehead, so quick that I didn't have a chance to react. It jostled the bruise under my eye.

"Four."

The palm of her hand began to warm up, like someone had put a wet teabag on my head.

"Three."

I hit her hand, trying to knock it off my head, but she swatted me away. Her hand was hot now, burning.

"Two," she said. "Tell me now or I'm ripping it out of your head."

"No."

"One."

CHAPTER 27

Away Message
Number1AvrillLavigneFanSoComplicated: If anyone has seen my brother Braden, please call! We are worried about him. He didn't come home last night, and I don't know what to do.

WHAT HAPPENED NEXT wasn't linear. Imagine my mind as a house, doors unlocked, windows open, and her as a team of burglars breaking into each of them simultaneously. I wasn't a person running around trying to lock it all down, but the house itself, clicking things shut, tensing muscles. I couldn't relax without her jiggling the latches again.

And then it was like being swarmed by bees. She attacked from so many places at once I couldn't block any one assault. I flailed, locking my mind away from her as best as I could, but then memories started playing. They floated out into the air, as though projected.

First, Sam throttling me, shaking my head back and forth. I saw it projected, and then I was in it, reliving that moment. His fingers are tight around my throat, my eyes are tearing up, I can't breathe. There's a blurry image of Mom and Dad. They sound so far away as they tell him to stop. My hand hits the table, and my fork bounces. Why don't they rip him off? But then he lets go and Dad is taking Sam away and Mom is taking me. She wants to how I provoked him.

Then, it's my conversation with Ancy from earlier that day. Me warning her. Her walking back into the store. But I'm not reliving the moment beat for beat, I'm reliving the pain. The shame of even considering Uncle Pauly's plan. And then I can feel the private investigator sneering at me. She's watching this too, and she's judging me.

And all at once, I knew that her name was Lorraine. I knew that she'd grown up in New Jersey, and that for her this was about the book. She'd known Screecher and hated him, knew that if he had the book he'd be doing the same thing that Uncle Pauly was doing, making a monster. She suspected that Pauly had killed the upstairs neighbor, sacrificing her to bring a monster onto this plane.

Then I pushed further into her head.

She'd been following Screecher the night he'd come to Joel's. Her memory projected, too, and then I was living the moment as her. She is on the highway following Screecher. He turns into a rest area. She parks far away from him, and she's watching people cycle in and out of the entrance. Then her car rocks back, and Screecher is behind her. He touches the back of her head and things go black.

It felt like a metal hook getting wrapped around my stomach. She yanked me out of her memory and now we're watching Uncle Pauly murder Screecher. There's a hint of sympathy, that a child shouldn't have to see that. Then we're at Uncle Pauly's apartment, in the closet with Paul Jr., and I experience her elation at having found what she was looking for digging through my memories.

Her emotions replace mine as we step through the closet door into the room. As the moss hits her nose, I feel her fear, an animal panic at the scent, what I feel when a cockroach crawls up my leg. And then my hand reaches back. When it hits the wall, I feel an exoskeleton, the word *FUCK* goes through my mind like a freight train.

Then we were both floating, the space black except for our bodies. We weren't wearing clothes, but weren't naked either. We were in a place beyond bodies. Our astral forms glowed blue, and she floated toward me, not swimming, but moving as if being drawn by a rope.

The house was gone. Whatever defenses I may have possessed were crushed. Her astral form touched my head, as her corporeal hand was touching my head in the real world. It was the world's worst carnival ride, disorienting, dizzying, and debilitating all at once. A kaleidoscope of colors spun around me and I spun too.

She was draining it all out of me, Uncle Pauly's sacrifice, Joel's plan, my failed love life.

But something stopped it. Her hand came off my head, as something knocked her back. Everything smelled like moss, it was there in my head. The monster saturated my brain, like it did in my dream. Lorraine taught me its name: Bryophyto.

CHAPTER 28

Away Message
bigRican787: If you want a job done right, sometimes you gotta do it yourself. Mom, if you're seeing this, Grandpa typed it! I didn't break my grounding!!!

IT WAS DARK and someone was shaking me. I closed my eyes again. I needed five more minutes. "Go away," I said, words slurred with sleep. I rolled over and tried to pull my pillow over my head, but instead I shoveled dried leaves into my face.

That someone shook me again. "I thought you were dead, dude."

I opened my eyes. A headache cleaved my skull in two. Joel stood over me. I oriented myself with the trees around me. The envelope. I scrambled, picking through my things but I couldn't find it. The camera was missing, too. "They're gone."

"What's gone? Are you okay?"

"Fine." My throat was desert-dry.

Joel shook his head. "Dude, you can't sleep back here."

"The private investigator?" I squinted. Even in the darkness the light felt like too much.

"I talked to her. She's on our side." He wiggled a finger under his cast to get at an itch. "She's buying us tickets to go into New York tomorrow."

Then I bolted awake. "Dude, you can't trust her." I was too weak to sit up. That mind-reading had kicked the shit out of me.

148

Joel helped me onto my feet. I stumbled, but he caught me. "You okay?"

"She did this to me." I took two steps toward his house, but fell onto my knees, almost dragging Joel down with me.

"Whoa there, pardner," he said.

"You can't go with her." She could mind-fuck him too. Or worse.

"She doesn't even need the book. She's going to take care of everything. And then all of this'll be over." He steadied me. My legs felt like jello.

"Don't trust her," I said. "She ripped it out of my brain."

"What's 'it'? How did she rip 'it' out of you?"

"Magic."

"Oh shit."

Joel yanked me off the ground and carried me into the house. His mom must've been at work because she didn't kill me for coming in while Joel was grounded. His grandpa must've been lurking somewhere, but I didn't see him. Joel threw me down on his bed, and I think he was going to talk to me about something, but I was out again before he got the chance.

That night in the dream apartment, I approached the cornucopia, the stench of Screecher's guts and the moss mixing into a malodor. I began to make out a shape.

The Bryophyto had to hunch to fit in the room. Its shoulders billowed out in either direction, broader than two men across, veiled in shadow. The monster rustled as it moved, bringing one arm forward, into the light. As it got closer, the moss smell intensified, almost overpowering the entrails.

Against my will, eyes closed. I pushed as hard as I could, trying to run, but I was paralyzed. It susurrated across the room, inching closer. Instead of escaping, I knelt and lifted the cornucopia.

Something heavy slid into the cornucopia. The monster slurped at the guts. Warm drops of Screecher's blood or bile or shit splashed me. If my body could've gagged, it would've. The walls of the cornucopia thrummed with the force of the monster's slurping. Another piece of it jammed itself into the cornucopia. Then a third bit, all vacuuming up Screecher's insides.

The Bryophyto made a noise, half a burp, half-chattering. Piece by piece, it removed itself. It rustled back into the shadows. I lowered the emptied cornucopia, only now feeling the burn in my shoulders from holding it up.

Something that looked like Paul Jr. came out from behind me. "He wants you to know."

I wanted to jump, but I still had no control.

I woke disoriented again, blinking the sunlight out of my eyes. I was in a bed, but it wasn't mine and I was lying across the foot of it. My head still ached, but rather than cleaved in two, it felt like a door jamb had been lodged in the middle. I managed to sit up, and saw the note Joel left for me next to a jug of Gatorade.

Dude,

I'm on my way into the city with the investigator. Stay hear and sleep. I'll take you home later.

Joel

Fuck. He was dead if I didn't get there.

"Joel, Braden's mom is on the phone," his mom yelled from the hallway. Her footsteps echoed toward his room.

I scrambled into the pile of dirty laundry on his floor

and rolled under the bed. I was face-to-face with my *Penthouse*. The centerfold hung out with a new stain in the center of the page.

Gross.

Joel's door swung open. "Is he here?"

From my vantage, I could only make out her feet. They were calloused from waiting tables, and a cotton ball was stuffed in between each of her toes while the fire-engine red paint dried.

I held my breath.

"Where the fuck is he?"

She walked out of the room.

Things were going to keep getting worse.

I waited for what felt like an hour. First bacon and then an egg sizzled against a griddle. I drooled. The smell was almost enough to send me running out there, consequences be damned. Thanks to Lorraine, I'd missed dinner.

When I heard Joel's mom start the water for the shower, I crawled out from under the bed and crept out into the hall. I had to tiptoe past the bathroom to get to the front door. When I saw it was cracked open, I paused. Why couldn't it be closed?

I had to hope the running water was loud enough to block out footsteps. I snuck toward the entryway and was almost at the door when her voice stopped me.

"Is that you, Dad?" Shit. I forgot about his grandpa.

If she saw me now, she'd suspect I'd been peeping on her in the shower and beat my ass the same shade of red as her toenails.

The central air cycled on, breezing the bathroom door shut.

I closed my eyes as I waited for the next noise. But it didn't come. I nearly plowed over Joel's grandpa on the steps.

"Braden," Joel's grandpa said.

I kept my voice low. "Forget you saw me."

"What?" he asked, shouting.

"She doesn't . . . " Then I stopped. Unless I screamed, he wouldn't hear me. So instead, I shook his hand and ran down the steps toward home.

Mercifully, there were no cars in the driveway. Inside, Leslie was at the kitchen table.

"Where were you?"

"Joel's." I didn't stop to chat.

She followed me up the stairs. "Mom and Dad are really worried about you."

"Where is she?"

"Picking up Uncle Pauly from the hospital."

"When did she leave?" I stopped in front of the door to my room.

"An hour ago."

Shit. They'd be back soon. "I need to borrow your bike."

She giggled. "Sure." Her bike was pink with purple streamers trailing off the handlebars. The manufacturer had painted a unicorn on the frame. "But let me get the camera first." I didn't bother telling her the camera was long gone. That was a tomorrow problem.

The room to Uncle Pauly's door was locked. "Stand back."

"What are you doing?"

I took her shoulders and steered her to safety. Then I kicked the door near the handle. It budged. I kicked it again. Pain shot up my leg, but I didn't care. If something happened to Joel, it would be my fault.

"Braden, don't." She balled her hands.

On the third kick, a crater formed around the doorknob, the white paint chipping up to reveal the cheap wood underneath. On the fourth kick, the door opened. I grabbed the book, and a backpack.

"Don't tell them I was here."

"You just kicked the door down!"

"I'll tell them why when I come back." I didn't say *if I come back*, but I thought it.

"Braden, you're scaring me." She tugged at my sleeve.

I went to my parents' room next, digging past the socks and condoms for Dad's emergency cash supply, and took five twenties.

"Braden, what are you doing?" Leslie cried out. She shoved me in the chest.

I hugged her. "I'll be back tonight. Tomorrow at the latest."

She shoved me again. "Where are you going?" She barred herself over the door.

"Move." I didn't have time for this.

"No."

I scooped her up and tossed her onto the sofa as she pounded on my chest. "I'll see you tomorrow."

Stone walls blocked off the yards of the houses on the narrow roads I had to ride down.

Traffic was fast, and one or two cars beeped at me. One guy rolled down his window to yell about me riding a girl bike. I kept on keeping on. I didn't have another choice. If Joel died, it would be my fault. He was my best friend. Getting hit by a car trying to save him would be better than losing him.

They were going to be at least a train ahead of me. But I didn't think there was enough magic in the world to wake Joel up early enough to catch an express train. Those had to get to the city with enough time for the commuters to catch a subway to their job.

Was Lorraine going to feed him to the Bryophyto? Would Lorraine turn him inside out, too? Would she choke him with the ropes that Screecher used on Uncle Pauly?

RYAN C. BRADLEY

My head was throbbing. I hoped the monotony of a train ride would lull my roiling brain into submission. I'd buy the biggest Gatorade they had at the station and something to eat. Maybe some Advil if they had it. And then I would conk out until reaching my destination.

Another car whooshed past. Finally, I made it downtown. The road I knew winded past the hardware store. I was glad Ancy wasn't there, or at least she wasn't working outside as I pedaled past. The last thing I needed, the only thing that could make this worse, would be her seeing me on Leslie's bike.

I don't know if every teenage boy is that silly, to worry about something so stupid during a life or death situation. But I know that I was. If I could go back and tell myself one thing, I'd say all the pressure to be a man will only rot away the parts of you worth saving.

At the station, I bought my ticket and enough empty-calorie snacks to make up for missing dinner and breakfast. I found a seat and ripped open a bag of Cheetos. I was ready to sleep my way into New York City. My stomach growled with excitement. I popped one into my mouth and nearly choked on it when Uncle Pauly and Sam stepped onto the train two cars up with Ancy in tow.

CHAPTER 29

Away Message
EnterSamMan88: This is so fucked. Impromptu
trip to vomit in NYC.

SO MUCH FOR SLEEPING. The only reason they hadn't spotted me was because their seats were facing the other direction. They sat Ancy in between them. Sam took the window seat, presumably so Uncle Pauly could hold her in. The train idled, doors open, giving other passengers time to board. How did they get her?

I ran a finger along the book's leathery skin in my backpack. What would happen if I stepped off the train with it? Would this all be over?

As I pondered, the train lurched forward. And then Sam climbed over Ancy and Uncle Pauly, hand over his mouth. He was going to need to run by my seat to get to the bathroom.

I grabbed my things and ran through the door between cars. The gap was uncovered. The first door had to shut before the second opened. For a moment, I was trapped in the wind, feeling the train's true speed. On the other side, I hooked into the alcove past the bathroom.

A woman in a pantsuit glanced up from her newspaper.

Sam burst into the bathroom.

After some guttural puking, he came out rubbing his stomach. I didn't know if I could trust him, but Mom had said that I had to take care of Sam. I called out to him as he opened the door between cars.

155

He turned, hair dancing in the wind.

The woman in the pantsuit put down her newspaper.

Sam stepped into the car. "Everyone is looking for you. Where have you been?" The door whooshed shut.

We didn't have time. "Does Uncle Pauly know I'm on the train? Did Leslie tell?"

Sam was green in the face, like he might hurl again. "You saw Leslie?"

She hadn't ratted me out. What a champ. "How did you get Ancy?"

"She was watering plants. Uncle Pauly grabbed her," Sam said. "I was still in the car. He told her if she screamed, he'd kill her family. This is fucked."

"Ahem. This is the quiet car," the woman in the suit told us.

Through the window of the next car, Uncle Pauly looked back. I flattened myself out of view.

"Sorry," Sam said. "I've got to get back, Bray. If I'm gone for too long . . . Is he going to do something to her?"

"I don't know. I think he is."

"He says this will get me off the waitlist," Sam said. "How?"

"I don't know. How did he do what he did to Screecher?"

The woman in the suit sighed. "*Quiet* car."

"Sorry," I said.

Sam wobbled back toward Uncle Pauly.

I waited until he sat before I took a seat near the back of the quiet car. The extra information left me more lost. All of it compounded into my headache. Whatever was good or bad for my family, I wasn't going to let Ancy get sacrificed. Joel either.

Uncle Pauly got up for Sam to pass, his fingers pressing into Ancy's bicep. When I was kid, he'd been the one to tell me never to hit my sister. He'd said a woman was like a flower—I should never bruise their petals. If Ancy lived, she'd have bruises for weeks from where he'd held her. She looked paralyzed with fear.

SAY UNCLE

I thought about what I would do if I were in her place. I pictured myself karate-chopping the hand off my arm. But even in my fantasy I wouldn't be strong enough. Uncle Pauly would punch me in the chest. I'd go down, and the escape attempt would be over. I hoped Ancy would be smarter, that she would bide her time.

My headache intensified with every bump. Fear spun through me, making my stomach feel like it was stuck in the metal blades of a blender.

Sam, Ancy, and Uncle Pauly were relatively still until we got to Grand Central. When the train pulled to a stop, I swung into a nook between windows until they walked past on the platform. Then I slipped out and followed them into the crowd.

Uncle Pauly's head stuck up like a shark's fin in the ocean of travelers. When I glimpsed Ancy through a crowd of armpits, her head was turning in every direction until she found what she was looking for. I followed her gaze to two men with assault rifles standing at the edge of the room. There'd been soldiers posted around the station since 9/11. Uncle Pauly saw, too, and he dragged Ancy away.

A man jostled me. "Watch it, pal!" he yelled, arms outstretched. I kept going.

One of the few advantages of being small was that I could slip through gaps in the crowd that other people couldn't. I drifted through, shifting to fit when I had to. My head throbbed, but at least my legs had resolidified.

Uncle Pauly guided Ancy toward the subway. I guessed a cab driver was more likely to notice a teenage girl being taken against her will. I couldn't believe any of the people around us weren't noticing the hand tight around her arm. But that was New York, I guess.

When they got to the stairs, Ancy stuck her leg between

Uncle Pauly's as he took the first step. He disappeared down the stairs to the first landing. Sam was on the other side of her, but he hurried to check on Uncle Pauly instead of grabbing Ancy. People yelled, maneuvering around Uncle Pauly. A few stopped, but most kept walking.

Ancy spun around and walked in the opposite direction like she hadn't been with him at all. Sam turned to chase her once he saw Uncle Pauly was okay, but the crowd swept him back. Uncle Pauly popped up, standing now with blood pouring out of his nose. An NYPD cop strolled over, thumbs jammed into his pockets.

Sam had lost track of her.

She might have gotten away if we hadn't locked eyes. She froze and Uncle Pauly's voice boomed through the commotion that he was fine.

Sam headed toward me, still not seeing Ancy. She stopped in front of me, eyes wide with panic. "Braden, you've got to help me."

"Run," I said.

Sam got to me before she had a chance to move. "Have you seen her?"

Ancy looked from me to him, facing dawning with recognition. "That guy was the one who bought the air conditioner. Your uncle."

Sam got to us before I could get her to run and grabbed her arm.

She jerked away, but Sam had her arm tight.

Then Uncle Pauly was there. "Hi, Braden." His hand was so quick, I didn't realize what he was doing until he'd cuffed my bicep, the same way he'd been holding Ancy. "C'mon, everybody. Time to take the train."

We had to stand on the subway. Uncle Pauly walked us into a corner. He grabbed a handhold in front of us, his giant chest blocking us from escaping. He could barely stand, but he was still huge. Sam was behind him, playing right field to Uncle Pauly's first base, though I doubted he would stop us if we got past Uncle Pauly.

"I'm going to kill your mom if you pull another stunt like that." Uncle Pauly was trying to sound calm, but he couldn't hide the anger underneath his words.

Ancy covered her mouth.

Uncle Pauly snatched my backpack. He jerked it open and smiled. "Glad to have it. No robe, though, huh?" Then he zipped the book away and hung the backpack over one shoulder.

My face turned red. I got angry like Mom, a deadly quiet coming over me.

"This is what it was all about," Ancy said, quietly. "Why you called me. Why you took me for ice cream."

I'd had one migraine in my life before Lorraine broke into my brain, and this was shaping up to be the third. It was like there was a pry bar pushing my brain into two directions, and every word pushed the halves further apart. "No." I willed back the hot tears welling up.

The truth was that Uncle Pauly had been manipulating me. No one had made me go through his things to get my *Penthouse* back. To take pictures of the pages and get them onto that forum. To drag Joel into this. But he'd introduced me to Ancy, coached me on how to act on our date, even if I didn't listen. He knew then that he'd sacrifice her. I mean, for fuck's sake, he called her a *practice girl*. I wanted to pull a Sam and throw up, but it wouldn't have been a relief. None of this pain would spew up. I couldn't look at Ancy, couldn't say any more.

I swallowed and blinked back the tears. "The private investigator is taking Joel to your apartment. She has your directions."

Uncle Pauly checked to make sure no one was listening. "What private investigator?"

"Lorraine. She was tracking Screecher. She has the envelope."

Uncle Pauly ran his hand through his hair. His shirt untucked, revealing a wet patch from the blood soaking through his bandage. "So you were on your way to fight Lorraine?"

"Where are you taking me?" Ancy shivered.

"Whoa." He craned down to squint at my forehead. Then he thumbed some hair away. "She broke into your mind. How are you standing?"

My headache swelled.

"I want to know where we're going," Ancy said, quietly, but with a confidence that demanded an answer.

Uncle Pauly didn't provide it. "You've either got some big balls or a small brain. Maybe both. She did that to you and you were going to fight her again?"

"Uncle Pauly, you're bleeding," Sam said.

"Tell me." Ancy stood up very straight.

Blood wet the top of Uncle Pauly's pants. He pulled up his shirt. The upper part of the bandage over his surgical incision was white, but the rest of it was oversaturated with blood.

He touched it, brought his fingers up to examine them, as if there were some debate as to what it might be.

He stuffed his shirt back into his pants. "We're almost there," he told Sam. Then he turned to Ancy. "You did this, you know. Tripping me on the stairs." If Uncle Pauly had a cliff, I thought he'd be at the edge of it, but he smiled. "You did a number on me. I wish it didn't have to be like this."

"Like what?" Ancy asked.

"He's going to sacrifice you," I said.

Her eyes went wide.

Uncle Pauly smacked me in the back of the head. "He doesn't know what he's talking about."

CHAPTER 30

Away Message
Number1AvrilLavigneFanSoComplicated:
Braden came back . . . and then left again!
At least he's okay for now, I guess??? :(

THERE WERE A lot of things wrong with Uncle
Pauly's apartment—drafts in the winter, heat in the
summer, noisy neighbors at the restaurant
downstairs year round—but you couldn't knock the
location. He lived less than a block from the subway,
spitting distance from Central Park.

His grip on my arm was weakening. Blood leaked from
his incision and soaked through his pants so it looked a
little like he'd pissed himself.

The maître d of Wolf Pho Vietnamese Fusion startled
when we came in.

"Afternoon, Mr. Martinez." She dropped her phone.
Her eyes widened. "Everything okay?"

"Hunky-dory," Uncle Pauly said, and hustled us all
toward the stairs. The vacant apartment was on the third
floor.

Ancy planted her feet. "He's kidnapping me. He's going
to kill me."

We froze. For a second, I believed Ancy had saved us.

"Excuse me?" the maître d said.

"I don't get kids' humor today." Uncle Pauly's grip
ratcheted iron-tight now, as he dragged us into the
stairwell.

"Call the police," Ancy yelled over her shoulder.

Uncle Pauly kicked the door into the stairwell shut behind him. The bloody hem of his shirt untucked again. "Even if she did call the police, they wouldn't get here on time. And now I have to kill your mom."

Ancy didn't answer him. She had a thousand-yard stare, looking into another world. Sam was the same way, moving like there was a fog disconnecting himself from what was happening.

Uncle Pauly had to pause at the first landing in the stairwell. His apartment and Aunt Linda were on the other side of that door. She'd stop him, really call the police. I jerked my arm, thinking to break free and get her out here.

Uncle Pauly used my momentum to slam me face-first into the door instead. I saw white. My headache screamed with the introduction of a new pain. "Goddamnit, Braden. Sam gets it."

Sam didn't seem too thrilled about it, though.

We went up the next flight, slowly. Uncle Pauly was suffering. I remembered him telling me about how he played through the high-school championship game with three broken ribs. Before every play, he'd told himself that he could do anything for thirty seconds. He must've been doing the same thing now, because we paused again at the next stairwell, on the level of the second apartment.

Uncle Pauly turned to us. "We're on the goal line. It's the fourth quarter. There's a minute left in the game. What you've got to ask yourself, can I dig deep enough to get this done? Am I the kind of man who follows through with the things he started?"

He didn't get the hoo-rahs he was expecting, but we continued to the apartment door.

"They're in there," I said.

"I know." Pain doubled Uncle Pauly over, but if anything it tightened his grip on me and Ancy.

"We could let her go home," Sam said.

SAY UNCLE

Uncle Pauly sneered at him. "After all of this, you think that lands us anywhere but a prison cell?"

"I wouldn't say anything," Ancy said. Her eyes came alive with desperation.

"See?" Sam asked.

"She's saying what you want to hear," Uncle Pauly said.

"What if you used magic to erase her memory?" Sam asked.

My head throbbed at the mention of magic.

"No, Sam. You gotta sack up, here. You want to go to Princeton, this is what gets you there." He brought himself back to his full height. The blood had soaked down to the knee now. "You want to be a rockstar, Bray, this is it. This is the ticket."

We walked down the hall, toward the door where Lorraine must've had Joel. Uncle Pauly trailed drops of blood. A thousand thoughts raced around my head at once, all about the different ways Lorraine could kill Joel. Slit his throat. Strangle him with those magic tendrils Screecher used. Reach down his throat and turn him inside out.

Uncle Pauly stopped again in front of the door. "Grab them," he commanded. Sam obeyed.

Ancy tested his grip right off the bat. She caught him with an elbow in the chest and he crashed against me, pinning me to the wall. I fell. She got two steps before he lunged. Then he had her good and tight. She groaned, thrashed against him, but he didn't let her go.

Uncle Pauly took the book from my backpack. He closed his eyes and pressed it to his forehead. Then he slapped himself in the face with it. He hopped up and down. Blood leaked out the bottom of his pants, puddling on the floor.

"Go time, motherfuckers."

CHAPTER 31

Away Message
BrayDay327: It's all my fault.

WE WALKED INTO the front room, greeted by a faint mossy smell. To the left, I caught my reflection in the mirror of the bathroom where his upstairs neighbor had died by "suicide" and shuddered. To the right, there was the closet that Paul Jr. had taken me through and that I'd visited again and again in my dreams since.

Ancy's face was set, a rock of determination.

Joel must have been freaking out, too, only a wall separating us. I listened hard, hoping to get any clue of what was happening to him. If he was still alive. But there was no noise.

The moss smell intensified with each step.

Sam's shoulders scrunched, like a scolded dog's.

The light glowed in the sheen of sweat on Uncle Pauly's face. With Sam holding us, Uncle Pauly applied pressure to the reopened incision. The pain made him hunch over. He clutched the book to his chest with his other hand.

We followed him without instruction. He signaled for us to stop outside the closet.

"Can we flank them?" Sam whispered.

Uncle Pauly shook his head. "If you go around, there's no gateway."

He bowed his head and said a few words in a language I didn't understand. Then he opened the closet door. The apartment reeked of moss now.

SAY UNCLE

"Everyone through," Uncle Pauly said.

Sam pushed me in first. I froze. I had been visiting this room in my dreams. Ancy struggled to break away at the entrance, but Uncle Pauly was there, blocking any escape route. Sam dragged her through. Uncle Pauly followed, shutting the door behind him. He bowed his head again, and whispered more in the other language. The crack of light at the bottom of the door disappeared.

Suddenly, in the other room, I could hear Lorraine speaking in that same language, loudly, unaware of our presence. I peeked out. Joel was buck naked, chained to the altar. His eyes were open, but there was something staticy about them, like his brain was tuned to a channel with no reception.

A giant shape loomed in the shadows. Lorraine talked to it, words that made no sense, all hard consonants. Vibrations shot went up my wrists from the cornucopia in my hands as the creature vacuumed Screecher's guts.

Ancy covered her mouth.

Sam gaped. "What is that?"

Uncle Pauly shushed them.

Its head, faceless leafy branches the size and shape of a watermelon, poked out of the shadows and turned sideways at Lorraine. Its behemoth shoulders stooped to fit inside the room. "She's asking it to eat your friend," Uncle Pauly whispered behind me. "She's seeing if it will accept another male sacrifice."

"Will it?" I asked.

"Not if I summoned it right," Uncle Pauly said.

"So you're going to feed me to that?" Ancy yelled. Her free hand came down fast and hard, breaking Sam's grip. She rocketed her knee into his groin. Sam squeaked and collapsed, releasing me as well.

Lorraine turned toward us. The Bryophyto did, too, the leaves of its body rustling as it moved.

"Fuck." Uncle Pauly stepped into the room.

Ancy opened the door we'd come in through. An

impossibly black void replaced the apartment on the other side. Ancy probed the darkness with her foot. There was nothing for her to stand on. She came back in and closed the door.

"You killed me, Braden," she said, voice tight with anguish.

"I warned you," I said, knowing that even if I saved her, it wouldn't be enough.

I ran to Joel. His eyes were vacant, the same way Paul Jr.'s were in my dreams. I slapped him to no effect.

Uncle Pauly stooped toward Lorraine. "It's mine."

The Bryophyto planted a fist into the floor, shaking the room. The arm came out of the shadows. First, I could only tell that it was green. And then I saw it was made up of a thousand roots and branches tangled and twisted into a limb. It didn't have fingers, but the green at the end of the arm stretched farther.

Joel was still frozen. The locks around his arms were cold. He had goosebumps all over from laying on the stone altar nude.

The monster's other massive arm rustled forward. The room shook as it propped up the monster's massive chest. The moss smell nearly knocked me down. The Bryophyto didn't have eyes, but it headed in Joel's direction.

Ancy stepped in front of the monster with one of the torches from the wall.

It stopped.

Uncle Pauly and Lorraine incanted at the same time. A golden tendril slithered out of Uncle Pauly's palm toward Ancy. Before it could reach, a torrent of flame blistered out of Lorraine's hand. Uncle Pauly jumped out of the way, tugging the golden tendril with him. The smell of her burning flesh seeped into the room.

The Bryophyto cowered from Ancy's torch. I couldn't free Joel, so I grabbed another torch off the wall and helped Ancy back it up, into the shadows. Electric fear flowed through me.

SAY UNCLE

Ancy nodded at me. We walked forward in unison.

Behind us, the tendril snaked across the floor. It caught Lorraine's foot and she crashed. Her next torrent of fire shot into the ceiling. Flaming plaster sprinkled onto our heads.The Bryophyto squealed. With no mouth, I had no idea how it made the sounds it did.

Instead of the apartment upstairs, there was only darkness on the other side of the smoldering hole.

I approached the behemoth from the left, Ancy from the right.

Uncle Pauly scratched a circle into the floor with his dagger and pressed a hand so it reached the other side of the portal above me. Water shot from his hand and extinguished my torch.

Uncle Pauly gave a command. The Bryophyto reared its head up, leaves rustling, and roared. It raised both its arms, knocking more of the ceiling loose. It pounded its fists on the ground then charged at me. I dodged it. Lorraine must've been distracted.

The behemoth barreled into her like a bus. She flew back and slammed into the wall behind her. Blood splashed out, from where I couldn't tell.

Ancy jammed the back of the torch into the Bryophyto. It went in easily, singeing the leaves black. The monster howled. Ancy stabbed again, leaving a steaming hole in its back. It reknit itself quickly, green leaves taking the place of the black.

Lorraine's arms and legs splayed at impossible angles. Two of her ribs poked through the skin, white spears smeared with blood.

The Bryophyto spun around, swinging, but it was slow. Ancy sidestepped it easily.

A cough racked Lorraine's dying body, speckling the floor with blood. Her top half came unstuck from the wall and flopped down. Pieces of the drywall stuck to her, leaving more of the room open to the void.

"Lady, bring us back to the real world or I'm dead too!" Ancy yelled.

The Bryopyto faced Ancy. I ran to the wall for another torch, but Sam grabbed my leg, tripping me. I kicked his hand off my ankle.

Uncle Pauly limped toward Ancy from behind.

I scrambled toward the wall. I commanded myself to have the courage of Ancy. To end this.

Sam got up and trapped me in a full nelson. "Bray, we can't stop this. You're making it worse."

"Ancy, look out!" I struggled, but Sam had the hold cinched in.

Ancy juked around Uncle Pauly, but he and his monstrous god cornered her. They backed her into the door into the next room. She opened it, but there was only void. Horror shriveled her.

"Lady, please," Ancy said.

Lorraine's glazed eyes turned brown. She whispered the command to open the gate. Suddenly the holes in the ceiling were in the floor of the apartment above. Ancy escaped into what was now another room of the apartment. The Bryophyto shambled after her.

"Follow her!" Uncle Pauly shouted. He hobbled toward the closet, trailing blood from his open incision.

Sam released me and ran ahead of Uncle Pauly.

"Where are my pants?" Joel asked from the altar, apparently awake now.

"Dude, not now!"

I charged Uncle Pauly. He was quick, though. With a single word, he had a golden tendril wrapped around my neck. It burnt, like touching a radiator, choking me.

"Braden, you can be upset all you want later." Sweat dripped down Uncle Pauly's face. The vessels in his eyes had popped, turning the white around his pupils red. "You start a job, you gotta finish the job."

In the next room, the apartment door opened. Aunt Linda squawked, "What the fuck is going on up here?"

CHAPTER 32

U NCLE PAULY'S GOLDEN ROPE disappeared.
I fell to the ground, rubbing at my neck, trying to
massage the air in and the burn off.

Uncle Pauly limped into the next room.

"Dude, you got to get my pants," Joel said.

I coughed. "Nobody gives a shit about your pants."

In my dumb teenage brain, Aunt Linda walking in
meant this was over. The arrival of a sensible adult signaled
that Uncle Pauly would have to stop this nonsense. The
Bryophyto would cease its impossible existence, the private
detective would stop being squished dead against the wall,
someone else would go through her bloodied pockets to get
the keys to let Joel out.

"Listen, Braden, there's a lighter and a travel-sized can
of hairspray in my pants."

"What?" I blinked a couple of times. My headache was
engulfing my ability to think.

"Like how we used to start fires. You said I couldn't
trust her." He signaled toward Lorraine, who'd folded onto
the floor. "There are some knives in there too. Give me the
keys and get in there. Stop your uncle."

Blood soaked through Lorraine's pants. The keys
would be sticky with gore, pasted in there.

"Pauly, what the fuck is this?" Aunt Linda shrieked in
the next room.

169

"No time to free you. Sorry, dude," I said. I found his pants, took the lighter and the spray can. I grabbed a torch off the wall. And I left Joel.

"I can explain," Uncle Pauly's voice echoed from the other side of the apartment. I hustled through the closet.

Aunt Linda stood opposite Uncle Pauly and Sam, who was struggling to hold onto Ancy. The Bryophyto was rustling in the other room, out of sight.

"Sam, you let that girl go this instant."

Sam released Ancy. She snapped toward Aunt Linda like a rubber band. She hugged the older woman, who awkwardly patted her shoulders.

"You're making a mistake," Uncle Pauly said. "You keep saying we need more. This is it. If I feed it, Pauly will go to the nice school on the upper-west side. You can open an art gallery or a bakery or whatever the fuck."

Aunt Linda rolled her eyes. She hadn't seen the monster yet.

"Just like a woman. This is what you asked for!"

"I didn't ask for anyone to die," Aunt Linda said, face turning pale.

"Cunt." He said something else in the other language. Then he muttered, "I'll just erase your memory after."

Before Aunt Linda could answer, the Bryophyto lumbered into the room. Ancy broke for the hallway. Uncle Pauly said another word in that language and the door slammed shut, trapping her.

"What the fuck is that?" Aunt Linda murmured. She rooted in place. Slack-jawed, staring at the monster.

I couldn't let this happen. I stepped in front of the Bryophyto again, torch between us.

Uncle Pauly recited another incantation, and the torch extinguished. His face grew more haggard, like the effort was sucking the life out of him.

The Bryophyto swiped me out of its way. The leaves of its arm brushed against me. Then the roots underneath sent me sprawling.

SAY UNCLE

I hit hard against the wall.

One of the Bryophyto's arm split into two. Each half wrapped around Aunt Linda's waist. The behemoth made a chittering noise. She stared up at it, too shocked or amazed at the monster in front of her to fight it.

Uncle Pauly made an angry noise. "No. Not her. The other one! The other one!"

But it was too late. Thorns sprouted out of the Bryophyto's arms. It tucked Aunt Linda's head to her chest, gently. The Bryophyto sawed its arm along her shoulder blades, tearing through flesh, muscle, bone, dragging its prickers back and forth. Aunt Linda moaned.

Uncle Pauly leafed through the book, searching for who knows what.

In another world, I would've blasted it from behind. In this one, I froze. I watched.

Sam wilted. He stumbled to the wall, then collapsed.

Ancy yanked at the closed door to no avail, crying.

Aunt Linda raised her head, slowly, until her eyes were level with Uncle Pauly's. He looked up from the book, to her. Her voice weak, she said, "You happy now?"

I came unstuck. I fumbled for the lighter, the spray can.

"It wasn't supposed to be you." He spiked the book. It bounced high in the air, pages fluttering.

The Bryophyto stuck an arm into the jagged orifice it had made. Aunt Linda's head fell back down. The Bryophyto slurped. Aunt Linda's blood and muscle were vacuumed through the leaves and branches making its arm. From the Bryophyto's faceless head, a sound emanated, a strange mix of a burp and a giggle, then a contented kind of chattering.

Uncle Pauly's face filled out. His wrinkles disappeared. His cheeks plumped. His knee, constantly bent from his football injury, straightened. "Not like this," he said, but he didn't stop the Bryophyto.

I sprayed the hairspray into its back. I flicked the lighter, again and again. It wasn't catching. Not now.

The Bryophyto ignored me as it worked its other arm into the hole in my aunt. Somewhere inside her, a bone broke with a wet crack. Ancy screamed. The second arm burrowed deeper, and the sound of the slurping doubled. It hoisted her up. Her arms dangled. The smell of her blood, her shit, her piss, mixed with the Bryophyto's mossy stench.

Uncle Pauly's hair lightened. The rings beneath his crying eyes disappeared. "Jesus, Linda."

And then the flint struck right. A flame whooshed, singeing the hairs off my finger, lighting into the Bryophyto's back. The leaves crisped. Then burnt. It wrenched its arms out of Aunt Linda, entrails splatting onto the floor. It reached back, toward the flames. What was left of Aunt Linda collapsed, blood pouring from the hole in her back.

"Braden, stop!" Uncle Pauly said.

The apartment rumbled as the Bryophyto fell to its knees. Its mossy stench was overtaken by the smell of it burning, like live wood in a fire. It squealed.

Uncle Pauly's footsteps pounded toward me. I spread the flames, circling the outside, watching the fire kindle, hoping it would keep burning after I'd stopped. Uncle Pauly slapped me across the face. My ears rang until I hit the ground, and then they erupted. The lighter and the can bounced out of my hands, tumbling in either direction.

But the flames were spreading along the Bryophyto's back. Uncle Pauly ripped off his bloodied shirt and tried to beat out the blaze. The Bryophyto flung him at the closest wall. It fell onto its face—or where its face would be if it had one—and let out another screech. The flames died down.

Ancy collected the lighter, then the hairspray. She had no problem with the flint. A plume of fire blasted into the prone monster.

The new flame sent the Bryophyto shuffling across the apartment. Glass shattered as it crashed through the window. Glass sprinkled the sidewalk below. It floated for a second, and then burst, its body poofing into so many bits of pollen. We ran to the window.

Instead of a flaming monster hurtling toward the ground, green wisps, little bits of moss, floated on the wind. Below the window, a Wall-Street type writhed on the ground, beating at the flaming bits of green that landed on him. A woman with a stroller fell to a knee, coughing. The baby wailed, protected by a cover.

Ancy pushed past me, to see the green sleeting the city. The remnants of the monster twirled in the wind. "Did we kill it?"

Uncle Pauly laughed. Crumpled in the corner. I had no idea how much of Aunt Linda's life force he had left. "You killed one. Thanks to Braden, every real man in America is building their own. There are millions of men building millions of monsters."

"Shut up," Ancy said. She scooped up the book and cradled it to her chest. "You're not getting this back. If you come near my mother, I'll burn this fucking thing."

He tried to stand, supporting himself against the wall. Whether it was all of the magic or the restoration, something had drained him. "Braden, stop her," he said.

They both looked at me, waiting to see what I would do.

I said, "Fuck you, Pauly."

CHAPTER 33

Text Conversation

(203) 710-xxxx: Can we get a coffee? I want to talk about some stuff. From when we were kids.

(203) 260-xxxx: Tuesday?

ON THE SIDEWALK, the woman had gotten up. The baby was crying. The Wall-Street type had his hands on his knees and he looked up at the window. He yelled something about calling the cops.

"We got to go, Braden," Ancy said.

"Would now be a good time to give me my pants?" Joel yelled from the other room.

"Oh shit," I said.

Ancy squeezed her hand into the dead woman's pocket for the keys. The locks popped easily. Uncle Pauly didn't try to stop us, he cradled Aunt Linda's body, laughing, refusing to look at her even as he held her upright. Her head was hanging on by a dangling piece of flesh. The hole in her back was a window, revealing a trail of sucked-clean bones into the muscle and organs the Bryophyto hadn't reached. Pauly had done this to himself, to her. Sam was passed out, and we made the unanimous decision that we couldn't carry him.

The three of us got out of there before the cops arrived. They passed us, a sea of sirens, as we hit the corner of the block.

174

SAY UNCLE

We flagged a cab and rode to Grand Central, the three of us silent. The cabbie glanced at our bloody clothes and threw back a towel. "Don't ruin my backseat." We dabbed ourselves as clean as we could.

My head ached the worst it ever had. I had to cover my eyes to stop the sunlight from getting in. I pictured my brain hemorrhaging, sending a spout of blood out through my nose, and I wished for it, if only it would relieve the pressure.

We stayed awake but silent in the cab. People at the station looked at us, and kept moving. Maybe they thought we came from a movie set. We waited a half hour, and when the train arrived, the three of us passed out. For the first time in weeks, I didn't go to Uncle Pauly's apartment. I actually slept.

I woke with Ancy's head on my shoulder. She was beautiful, and I couldn't believe that she trusted me this much. That she was so willing to snuggle up. I thought it meant she forgave me. I wanted to cry right then, over what had happened to Aunt Linda. Over what had happened to Ancy. Over what had happened to Screecher and Lorraine. But I also wanted to shout, to run up and down the aisle of the train whooping so everyone knew that a girl could love me.

She blinked twice when I shook her awake at Milford. She slipped her hand out of mine when I tried to hold it. I had to walk fast to keep up with her, which wasn't easy given the fissure of pain in my brain.

"Ancy," I said, as we approached the hardware store.

She turned toward me, book against her stomach.

"Would it be okay if I called you?"

Ancy closed her eyes and bit her lip.

"What's wrong with you, Braden!" Joel shouted.

People on the sidewalk gawked at us.

"Your uncle tried to kill me," she said.

"I saved your life." My cheek throbbed, and it somehow made my headache worse. I winced.

"You saved my life? You dragged me into this, into your screwed-up family's problems." Her arms flailed as she spoke.

I hadn't thought of it that way.

"I want you to lose my phone number. If I see you in the store, I'm going to take one of the chainsaws off the wall and cut you in half. Same goes for your uncle and your brother."

Her words rocked me. I went to follow her, but Joel grabbed my arm. He sat me down on a bench on the city green. The crowd died down after a minute or two. I didn't know how I'd fucked things up so badly. It occurred to me then that she'd fallen asleep on me out of pure exhaustion.

Jesus Christ, I had fucked things up.

Joel draped an arm over my shoulders. "You're a fucking idiot, Bray. But guess what?"

I sighed. "What?"

"I'll still be your friend."

I stared at the Subway across the street, fantasizing about a meatball grinder when my parents walked by, Leslie in tow.

Mom was somehow angrier than she'd been this morning, past the nuclear quiet and onto a level of anger I'd never seen before. Dad's shoulders were slumped. Leslie was crying. She took a few steps, and then she'd stop until Mom yanked her arm again.

Leslie spotted me across the street and pointed. Then the three of them were coming over to our bench. All at once, they volleyed questions.

Mom: "Where were you?"

Dad: "What happened to your shirt?"

Leslie: "How could you leave Sam?"

Mom: "Didn't we raise you better than this?"

Dad: "Were you at Uncle Pauly's?"

Leslie: "How could you leave Sam?"

Mom: "Do you know how much trouble you're in?"

Dad: "Are you okay?"

SAY UNCLE

Leslie: "How could you leave Sam?"

They didn't leave time for me to answer anything, but I asked a question of my own. "What are you doing here?"

Mom put her hands on her hips. "We're going to the police station. Pauly and Sam have been arrested."

"There were three dead bodies with him," Leslie said.

I saw Aunt Linda's husk, Lorraine's crumpled sack. "Who's the third?"

"Who are the three? Who did they kill?" Joel covered his mouth with his casted hand.

Dad squeezed onto the bench next to Joel. "Ana, you go ahead to the police station. I'll fill them in."

"Were they there?" Mom asked.

This time, we answered together, "No."

"Great," Mom said. She stalked off, tugging Leslie behind her.

"Who was dead?" I asked.

Dad sighed. When his uncle died, he'd said it as a special intention at the end of grace instead of telling us directly. I don't think he knew yet—I didn't know—that what had happened that afternoon would scar me for the rest of my life. There'd be panic attacks near mossy smells, random crying, punching holes in walls. I had seen Aunt Linda and Lorraine die in that apartment. Most people were lucky enough to go their entire lives without witnessing such intense atrocity.

"You know," Dad said. "Sometimes bad things happen to good people. It's not anybody's fault."

But it was. It was Uncle Pauly's fault. "Just tell me, Dad."

"Your aunt Linda," he said.

"Who else?" I asked, maybe too quickly. Maybe I should've reacted, but I'd watched the Bryophyto suck the life out of her and into Uncle Pauly. I knew she was dead but it was too soon for me to feel it.

Dad sighed. "I know it's hard. Things were bad between your uncle Pauly and her—"

177

"Who else?"

Dad paused. He wasn't hearing me, though. "We all still loved Linda."

"Who else was dead?" Joel asked.

"I don't know." He took off his glasses so he could rub his eyes. "Sam called us from the police station, and from what I could tell was that he didn't know the other two people. We think one was that guy from the news. The senator's son who disappeared."

"Was Sam alone?"

"I'm not sure who else was there," Dad said. He took off his glasses to wipe his eyes.

"How are you holding up, Mr. O'Riley?" Joel put his other arm over Dad, cast and all.

"Oh jeez," Dad said. "Your mom called this morning. She's looking for you. She's beyond worried."

Joel rubbed Dad's back. "Could you give me a ride home?"

With Uncle Pauly and Sam out of the house, I could've taken back my bed. I could've slept in Sam's while he recovered in the hospital. It was all too good for me. I chose the husk of the air mattress, not even bothering to fill it. I pressed through the mattress onto the hardwood floor whenever I rolled, but I didn't care.

Again, I slept actual restful, dreamless sleep. The Bryophyto's hold on me, or whatever it was, was broken. The headache from Lorraine ripping through my brain finally passed when Leslie kicked me awake. "Get up. Sam's on his way home," she said.

I lifted my head. I felt like I needed another day of sleep, maybe two. Leslie kicked again. "You've been sleeping since Tuesday."

"What day is it?" I blinked again and again. My eyes weren't adjusting to the afternoon light.

"Thursday," she said.

I went downstairs and made a roast beef and cheddar sandwich slathered with BBQ sauce. I ate it, and then another. And a third. I drank a pitcher of water. I ate a package of grapes. Then I made my way through half a carton of chocolate ice cream. I would've kept eating if Sam hadn't come in.

He had a vacant expression, like he didn't know what was happening around him. Dad was leading him by one arm, Mom by the other. Sam brushed them off when he saw me.

"Bray," he said.

I thought he was going over the cliff, but instead he hugged me.

"It's going to be okay," he said.

For a couple of weeks, Maria and Paul Jr. stayed with us. I waited for someone to ask me what happened, for the police to find my fingerprints or Joel's. But the DA never filed charges against Uncle Pauly "due to a lack of evidence." He must've been one of those million men Pauly had gifted with his spell. Then Uncle Pauly planned the funeral.

I'd said that I didn't want to go, but there was no negotiating. Anyway, I loved my cousins and Linda had been their mother. She'd been the only person I'd ever seen call Uncle Pauly on his bullshit. She hadn't been afraid. So I got on another Metro North train to the city. We drove by the hardware store where Ancy was again out front, watering the hanging flowers.

"Do you want to stop so we can say hi?" Dad asked.

"No," I said, and I sunk deeper into my seat, putting a hand in front of my eyes to block her from noticing me. I'd hurt her enough.

179

We had to wait in the receiving line. Mom and Uncle Pauly had five other siblings, and we had thirty-three cousins, all of who were floating around the room, some in line, some already through it catching up. The whole family only got together for Christmas and funerals, which made death feel strangely festive.

Uncle Pauly stood at the front of the line, standing taller, like the hitch in his knees that had hobbled him had gone. His hair had a lot more pepper than salt. His hairline had thickened. There was a smirk, lurking underneath his obviously forced mourning face.

It contrasted with Maria and Paul Jr. Maria consoled her younger brother, as he cried. I reminded myself that I was doing this for them, and I stepped forward in line.

When it was my turn, Uncle Pauly smiled. "Braden, it's good to see you."

I wanted to shout, to scream, to yell, to tear my shirt open. More than anything, I wanted to tell everyone that he'd done it. He'd killed Aunt Linda. He put a hand on my shoulder, gently. His sleeve slid down. Light glinted off a solid gold watch band.

"I told you it would all work out if we just pushed through," he said.

For years, I swallowed my pain, kept Uncle Pauly's secrets. Because no one would believe me. Because that's what I was supposed to do. To watch as Sam got into Princeton, ascended through the world of high finance. To hold my tongue as Dad got promoted well beyond his abilities. To see Paul Jr. star as a young heart throb on a CW show. To accept the opportunities that came my way, the scholarship to a small local college. These things fall into the men's laps, while Mom and Leslie and Maria got nothing of their own.

Once in a while I check on Ancy's Facebook page. She ended up becoming a third grade teacher, not a lawyer. She has a golden retriever she seems to love. There's no sign she's using the book. Maybe she destroyed it. Maybe she has it somewhere safe. I hope she never thinks about it.

I saw Sam a week before I wrote this. He's gotten older, hairline hinting at receding. His body type has shifted over the years, with the veins in his arms becoming more pronounced as he cuts his body fat percentage lower and lower.

We never really talked about what had happened in Uncle Pauly's apartment that day, but over hot drinks in a midtown coffee shop with a cup of joe painted on the window, Sam brought it up. "Was it all worth it?"

I think I'd thought about it more than him, because my answer came quickly. "No," I told him. "Aunt Linda deserved better. Even Lorraine and Screecher, they didn't deserve that."

Sam nodded, slowly. His face was unmoving. His violent younger years have transformed into a tranquil adulthood. "Is it our fault?" he asked.

This time, I had no answer. I didn't turn away the advantages, even as I knew where they came from. All I had to do was sit down and shut up.

Sam looked into his coffee for a long time. Then, finally, he changed the subject, "Do you think the Giants are going to be any good this year?"

We hugged on the way out, professed our love for one another.

I went home and wrote this in a trance. I'm standing up. I'm speaking out. These are our secrets. My family is going to hate me for writing this. It will be worth it if you hear me. Please hear me.

ACKNOWLEDGEMENTS

I'll start out by thanking my amazing family. There was some concern that people would read *Say Uncle* and think this was a portrayal of what my life was like growing up. It's not. My father worked long hours, yes, but after he volunteered as an assistant soccer coach and Boy Scout leader. My mother was the opposite of neglectful, attending every sports game and award ceremony and other things that I've long forgotten, but with her insane memory she probably knows the exact time and date of all of them. And at each event, she brought so many apples. My brother Bill has never been waitlisted from anything his entire life, and he's always wanted to see the best out of me. My sister Katie has been an excellent sounding board and has always been there when I needed someone to talk to. The family you see on these pages is not them, though they served as inspiration for these characters.

Likewise for Uncle Pauly. I imagine a couple of my uncles may see themselves in this character, but he's not you. He's inspired by the idea of what would it have been like if Uncle Buck was evil.

I'd like to thank the city of Milford, where I spent twenty-five or so years growing up. I know the hardware store and the police station aren't across the green from each other (or even on the green in the case of the police station), but I had to shift some things around to have Uncle Pauly be able to snatch Ancy close to the train station and for Braden to see her across the street when he goes in for questioning.

A huge thank you to Max Booth III and Lori Michelle Booth for their work editing, formatting, and publishing this book. The book is so much better with the edits! When I started writing *Say Uncle*, the dream was that Ghoulish (Perpetual Motion Machine Publishing still, at that time) would publish it. I couldn't be happier that it's now a reality.

Luke Spooner knocked it out the park with this cover!

Another huge thanks to two groups of writers. The first is my writing group, The Word Shed, who went through with me one chapter at a time. Jenny, Johnnie, Steven, Lynne, Lorna, Donna, JayCee, and David for going through this with me chapter by chapter and helping make it the strongest book I could write. The second is my Texas Horror Crew: L.P. Hernandez, Agatha Andrews, Grace Reynolds, Celso Hurtado, R.C. Hausen, Johnny Compton, R.J. Joseph, Miguel Myers, Zach Chapman, Andrew Hilbert, Lucas Mangum, Susan Snyder, John Baltisberger, and Michael Louis Dixon. I'm sure I've forgotten someone, but you all are the best writers, and more importantly the most fun people!

Another huge thank you to Chris Poole, Cass Clarke, Chuck Hewitt, and Samantha Edington, first readers of so much of my work. If I'm any good, it's because of you.

And lastly, (which I feel the need to point out is also most importantly), to Betsy, Sydney, and Kajal. I love the three of you so much. There'd be no book without you. There'd be no me, or if there was, he'd be shining apples at a grocery store somewhere.

All love,
Ryan

ABOUT THE AUTHOR

Ryan C. Bradley (he/him) is a musician, podcaster, and the author of *Saint's Blood, Bad Connections: Horror Stories*, and co-author of *Dumb Bullshit for Brilliant Idiots*. His short fiction has appeared in *NoSleep, Tales to Terrify*, and *Dark Moon Digest* among others. He co-hosts *Horror Hangover* with Cass Clarke. You can learn more about him at ryancbradley.com.

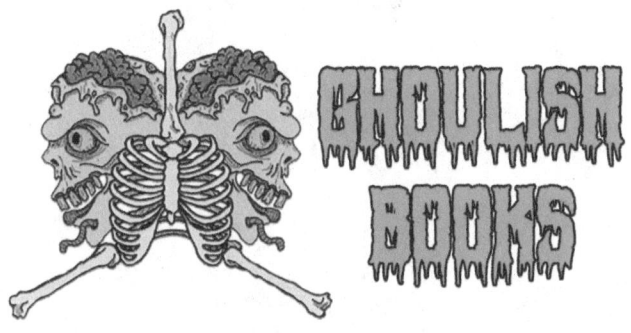

Patreon:
www.patreon.com/ghoulishbooks

Website:
www.Ghoulish.rip

Facebook:
www.facebook.com/GhoulishBooks

Bluesky:
@ghoulish.bsky.social

Instagram:
@GhoulishBookstore

Linktree:
linktr.ee/ghoulishbooks